DESTINY'S DARK LIGHT

Sara Dobie Bauer

Pen and Kink Publishing

Pen and Kink Publishing
www.penandkinkpub.com

Publisher's Note: This is a work of fiction. Names, characters, places, and incidents are a product of the author's imagination. Locales and public names are sometimes used for atmospheric purposes. Any resemblance to actual people, living or dead, or to businesses, companies, events, institutions, or locales is completely coincidental.

Book Layout © 2014 BookDesignTemplates.com
Cover design by BZN Studios
Edited by Cori Vidae

Destiny's Dark Light/ Sara Dobie Bauer. -- 1st ed.
ISBN 978-1-988233-66-6 (Physical)
ISBN 978-1-988233-67-3 (Electronic)

DESTINY'S DARK LIGHT

CONTENTS

Time will come for Loach and Dorcha to meet,
but divining when is no easy feat.
Born enemies, the Loach shall harness magic light,
while Dorcha brings about eternal night.
The Dorcha will have eyes of green and blue,
while Loach will shine bright of hue.
When they finally meet and their powers awaken,
the magic world will be mightily shaken.
Our people hope for light magic to triumph,
But wishing against fate is an act of defiance.

—THE BOOK OF SHADOWS

Chapter One

Cyan Burroughs reclined in the rickety leather chair that smelled of sage with her big, black boots propped on the desk edge. The dim morning light of her aunt Sybil's secret office was more than enough to read by as she flipped through another dusty tome about spell casting until the pungent odor of painting oils crept up behind her. She turned to find Sybil—red hair in a halo of frizz and a smudge of black on her nose.

"What are you doing here already?" Sybil asked.

"I never went home last night." Cyan closed the book and tossed it on the desk. They both coughed on a cloud of spilled incense ash.

From behind her back, Aunt Sybil pulled a small canvas and handed it to her niece. "I'm quite proud of this one. Finished it after breakfast this morning."

Cyan sighed and looked down at the black and white painting—one of dozens her aunt had crafted over the years, never in color, because Sybil's visions were never in color, as if the fates wanted her aunt's psychic ability relegated to the silent film era.

The painting was of *him* again. Cyan had known his face since infancy, the man her aunt said she would one day love. This particular painting was of him in profile, sun shining across his dark hair and casting shadows down his handsome face.

"It looks like every other one you've done." Cyan handed the painting back. She grew tired of his image sometimes, tired of waiting for him to show, tired… just tired.

Cyan jokingly called *him* "Dofheicthe," Gaelic for "invisible"—"Dof" for short.

She laughed off all the paintings and Sybil's promises of true love but secretly kept a folded piece of paper in her wallet—a tiny drawing of his face penned when Cyan was only thirteen, back when she believed fleetingly in princesses finding Prince Charming.

Sybil sighed through her nose and studied the small canvas. She sang, "Someday, my prince will come…"

Cyan yawned and stood. She used the rubber band on her wrist to pull her nappy blonde braids into a huge ponytail on the back of her head and walked to the bookshelf behind the midnight blue curtain, where Sybil kept the real treasures. Most people didn't know about the secret books behind the blue curtain—books about curses, spells, and the Craft. They may have suspected, but they didn't *know,* excepting a choice, old money few. Just as most people didn't know members of the Plainacher-Burroughs clan were actually witches, Cyan's father included.

Sybil owned a popular bookstore on Broad Street in downtown Charleston, South Carolina, known simply as Sea Books—an oceanside play on her abilities as a seer—and lived in the small apartment upstairs. People often came for Sybil's books on natural remedies and self-help, while Cyan's mother, Rue, taught classes about tinctures and anti-aging creams.

"Did you sleep at all, sweetheart?"

Cyan dismissed her aunt with a hand wave and fingered through spell books until she found one about potions.

Sybil muttered to herself and disappeared back to the front of the bookstore, leaving behind the smell of honeysuckle, a scent that heightened psychic awareness. Cyan resumed her position at the desk and kept reading; she couldn't do anything else.

Cyan's destiny had been determined while she was still in her mother's womb—her powerful Grandmother Plainacher sensed that she would grow to be the Loach, the witch prophesized in her people's *Book of Shadows* to take down the dark Dorcha, and Sybil backed her mother's bid. So Cyan was born to fight, it seemed, but in the long history of her family's magic, she was the only one who had not manifested during puberty.

The prophecy stated her powers would lie dormant until the appearance of the Dorcha. No matter how many potions her mother mixed, how many blood-bound spells her father cast, Cyan was defenseless in a world that expected her to one day be its protector. She toyed mindlessly with the black agate pendant at her throat.

"Go get me some hot chocolate, dear," Sybil's voice said from the front room. "You know how I like it."

"Dark with heavy cream and two sugars," Cyan grumbled, although maybe it was indeed time she saw the sun.

Liam Cody sat up in bed and stretched his long arms. The sunlight streamed in through the blinds and touched his eyes. He always woke with the sunrise, always—the life of a habitual runner. Just as he went to stand, though, he felt Zoe's arms wrap around his waist and pull.

"Stay," she said.

He kissed the top of her head. "I want to run five miles today."

"Run five miles tomorrow."

"Tomorrow is Saturday. And if this fundraising event tonight promises as much champagne as you keep hinting at, I plan to spend tomorrow in my pajamas between sessions of lazy sex and bad television."

She sighed and rolled back over.

They'd only been in Charleston for three weeks, ever since Zoe landed the job at a posh all-girls school, teaching English. Together, they'd packed their belongings in San Francisco and hit the road. They'd been lucky to find a two-story house in the French Quarter, chopped into sizeable condos. Then, Liam found a job as manager of the Broad Street Bistro, the most high-end steakhouse in a town of high-end restaurants. Sometimes, he felt like his life had been nothing but blessed since he met Zoe three years ago in that wine bar on the coast.

He ran a little over five miles that morning. The weather was so different in Charleston—such a change from the foggy west coast. Even though it was November, the humidity still stuck, but so did a cool breeze. He arrived home soaking wet with sweat, which made Zoe squeal when he tried to hug her. After she headed off to the exclusive Brighton School for Girls, Liam showered, shaved, and watched the BBC news, his favorite, before thumbing through his extensive wardrobe of very expensive suits.

He was a clotheshorse, but it was part of the job. He'd been working in high-end restaurants since arriving in America from Ireland when he was eighteen. His job was about organizing inventory and scheduling staff, but more so, it was about charming the customer—and looking the part.

He chose a specially ordered Spencer Hart navy blue suit with a light blue shirt and navy tie. He made sure his shoes were extra shiny, gave a quick glance at his tuxedo hanging on the closet door—which he would need for Zoe's school event that night—and stepped out into a morning that smelled of salt and seafood.

Broad Street Bistro was only a few blocks from their condo, so he made it there by nine, as planned. Broad Street was, arguably, the most beautiful street in his new southern home, what with its towering palm trees, antique architecture, and red brick road. He wandered past shops, still closed, and pulled keys from his pocket as he approached the huge, darkened window of the Bistro.

As he moved to unlock the door, though, someone bumped into him and didn't stop or apologize. Liam dropped the keys but watched a wild, lengthy mass of bright blonde braids swinging away from him. The woman had a book in one hand and a Styrofoam cup in the other. She wore an aged leather jacket and tight, black jeans. She couldn't have been more than five-foot-five—a tiny thing compared to Liam—and she had the tight little body of a woman who'd be fun in bed.

"What's up, bro?" Tommy, the sous chef, arrived at his side and joined him in admiring the view as the distracted blonde woman wandered further down Broad. "Hey, don't you have a hot chick at home?"

Liam smiled and shoved Tommy in the shoulder. "Window shopping, little man. Just window shopping." He reached down and picked up the dropped keys.

"Who you calling little?"

Liam stood and held the keys above his head. "Get the keys from me."

Tommy shook his head and laughed. "Ass. Let me inside. Let's get this day started. You know we have a twenty top tonight?"

"I heard," Liam said as he unlocked the huge, wooden front door. "I won't be here. I have a swanky fundraiser thing for Zoe's school."

"Lucky bastard."

Inside, the Bistro carried the lingering scent of melted butter and wood polish. Liam stared up the grand staircase that led to not one but two additional stories. The liquor bottles downstairs glowed dim shades of orange as the sun made its entrance down the center of Broad Street outside.

Liam sighed. "Gotta love the south."

Rue walked into Sea Books around lunchtime in a flowing skirt and peasant blouse, which meant she was trying to cover…

"You can't just walk around Charleston barefoot, Mother," Cyan said as she lounged in an old chair, yawning and reading a book about astral projection.

"You, young lady, wear combat boots in August. You are not one to judge."

Cyan sighed into the book's binding and considered a nap.

"Rue!" Sybil's soft voice emerged from the secret back room, and she soon made an appearance, her red hair a mess. She leaned forward and kissed her elder sister twice on the cheeks. "What's all this?" She gestured to three canvas bags Rue carried gracefully on her shoulders.

"Oh, I thought I'd get a jump on that skin treatment class this weekend." She dropped one bag at a time, a couple overflowing with dried flowers.

Cyan didn't have any use for skin treatments and anti-aging potions, but she *knew* they worked just from looking at her mother, over forty and not looking a day over twenty-eight.

Cyan got her blonde hair and gray eyes from her mother. She got her attitude from her daddy, Drake Burroughs—a construction worker with massive strength and a touch of the dark side to his magic. Drake could have gone either way: light witch or dark. He said it was her mother's love that kept him good.

Rue eyed her daughter's lax pose. "Slow day today?"

"It'll pick up. You know it always does, especially with your herbal remedy class coming up."

As if Sybil's prescient words beckoned the bell on the door, it rang, and a woman in a white pantsuit and black fur entered, removed her sunglasses, and gave the shop a sniff.

Sybil moved into action, smiling in that gentle way of hers. "Welcome, Mrs. Wagener. How are you this beautiful morning?"

Cyan thought the rich woman could use some of Rue's skin treatments, but it might be too late. She'd ruined herself with plastic surgery. Her face was shiny from over-stretching and her eyebrows raised in a constant state of surprise.

Mrs. Wagener tucked her sunglasses into a massive leather purse. "It's about my husband. Rue, I am indeed pleased to see you, child."

Rue crossed her arms. "Oh, I am sure, Elizabeth." She gestured to Sea Books' back room. "Come on."

Cyan went to follow, but Sybil put her hands on her niece's shoulders. "You watch the front of the shop, dear. I'll help your mother."

"But—"

"Sweetheart." Sybil touched one of Cyan's braids as her brow furrowed. "You don't have the touch yet. Just stay out front and help any customers, all right?"

Cyan sighed and sat back down on the couch, resting her elbows on her knees. "Stupid prophecy," she muttered as her aunt disappeared behind the midnight blue curtain. She leaned back in her chair and thought about what the astral projection book had been saying—about incantations and rising from the corporeal form. She folded her small, pale hands on her stomach, took a deep breath, and thought about rising out of her body, but all that did was make her fall asleep.

By the time Rue and Sybil returned with Mrs. Wagener, Cyan had slept a good forty-five minutes. She watched her beautiful, blonde, barefoot mother usher the rich woman to the front door and wave her out into the street. Then, Rue turned and sat on the arm of Cyan's chair.

"What was all that about?"

Rue looked at Sybil, and they both chortled.

"What?"

"Well, as you know, Mr. Wagener isn't the best looking of gentlemen, although I'm assured his pocket book is something to see." Rue rolled her eyes. "She wanted us to decrease his libido."

Sybil giggled into the palm of her hand, covered in rings of different stones.

"God, why would you want to do that to your own husband? As I understand it, sex is supposed to be fun."

"Oh, honey," Rue said, "not all men have the animal magnetism of your father."

Cyan winced. "Gross."

"Maybe if you tried dating—"

Cyan cut her mother off with a groan. "We've talked about this. I'm not putting some man in danger prior to the War just because you want me to lose my virginity."

Rue winced and looked a lot like her daughter. "I'm not talking about… Christ Almighty, Cyan, can't we just have a conversation about boys? There must be some on this peninsula you find attractive. Unless you don't like boys?"

"I like boys," Cyan barked.

"Of course she does," Sybil agreed. "No way you've forgotten the beautiful man that's her destiny, Rue."

"Please don't make it sound like we're in a Disney movie," Cyan spat.

"Oh!" Sybil clapped. "Let me show you the most recent painting!" She dashed to the back room, where she kept all her paintings of Cyan's supposed true love.

"Any sign of the Dof?" Rue asked.

"I'm not ready, and it's not time. You know it's not time."

"He might show up before the War," Rue said. "Then, what'll you do?"

Cyan curled a long braid around her fingertip. "Keep him safe," she whispered.

Chapter Two

Liam looked at his reflection: dark hair in an idyllic swoop, clean shave from his trusty—and old-fashioned, perhaps—straight razor, and green eyes sparkling like the Emerald Isle where he was born. He adjusted his black bowtie in the mirror: checking its proper alignment had almost become a nervous tic.

"It's straight." Zoe appeared reflected behind him. She set a glass of red wine on the counter. "You are so OCD."

"I'm not OCD," he said to her retreating back. "It's just always crooked in pictures."

He grabbed his wine glass and took a sniff. Previously trained as a sommelier, he recognized a California Cabernet by smell alone.

Tonight would be his first meeting with all Zoe's co-workers from the fancy private school where she taught. Earlier they'd gone over the list of things not to discuss—including but not limited to gay rights, Paula Deen, and Catholicism—and Liam felt oddly insecure. He was about to meet some of Charleston's poshest, and he was just a bar manager. Granted, at one of the most expensive restaurants in town, but still just a bar manager.

Liam stopped fiddling with his tie and noticed the evening outside the window glowed gold. He felt so alive in Charleston—magnetic almost, as if he could do anything there. The town really did seem to shimmer, and the nights smelled like lilac. He was peacefully enjoying his wine's oaky bouquet when the spike of pain hit, right across his temple, behind his eyes. He gasped and bent forward.

The pain was like the scorch of burnt flesh—only inside his brain. He crushed his eyes shut and pressed on his forehead as if he might be able to push the agony away. Slowly, it dwindled, until he was able to breathe. Luckily he hadn't dropped his wine glass and Zoe had already left the room. His headaches upset her, and it upset her even more when he said they were "nothing."

He joked about having a brain tumor—well, it was sort of a joke—because he actually didn't know anything about his family health history except that his mother died of some kind of cancer and his father a heart attack when Liam was no more than a toddler. He came from money, lots of money, which was why he attended high-end boarding schools until the age of eighteen, when he decided to run away and start over in America, in California.

He found his niche there in the food world, working his way up from dishwasher to manager to sommelier. Then, he met Zoe. He was drawn to more than her beauty and intelligence. She was an orphan, too. Her parents died in a house fire that happened while Zoe was away, having a good time at a sleepover birthday party, unaware her life was being destroyed. Unlike Liam, her family didn't have money, so she spent much of her childhood lonely in a Catholic orphanage like some Broadway musical travesty.

Sometimes he thought their shared fear of being left alone—again—made them desperate for each other. There were nights when their lovemaking felt more like cannibalistic clawing than pure passion, as if when her nails drew blood on his back, she reminded herself that he was real and alive. When she bit at his chest, she perhaps sought his heartbeat. He had similar affectations. In the middle of the night, he occasionally reached out half expecting to find her body cold, her soul departed. When he found her warm and breathing instead, he laid as close as possible to simply feel her heat.

Yes, perhaps broken people fit together like puzzle pieces. Liam abandoned his wine on the bathroom sink and went to kiss the woman he hoped might one day be his wife.

At 6 PM sharp, Sybil forcibly removed her niece from Sea Books, claiming, "You must eat and sleep like a normal person." Only in Cyan's family would "normal" sound like such a horrible thing. The city was almost dark with the descending late autumn sun as she walked down Broad Street. It was packed with people trying to get home from work or downtown to bars. Cyan kicked at loose rocks on pavement and tried not to run into anyone.

She wouldn't have noticed the dark figure lurking in the alley ahead if not for the minute glow of red oozing from beneath his long, black jacket. She couldn't see his face but, when he raised his hand, she saw the glow came from his very skin.

She'd seen things like that before in her own household—all witches projected their own individualized colors. This was something else, though, something that made her shout, "Hey!" People turned to look at her, as did the man with the glowing red hand, but her call was too late. The force of his power erupted over the street like a volcanic tidal wave and then, chaos.

A peaceful green trolley, filled with businesspeople and tourists, flew straight off the pavement and high into the sky. It landed with a horrible screech, crashing down on several cars below. People screamed and ran, but Cyan remained calm and looked to the man in the black cloak. He had, of course, disappeared.

"Shit," she hissed.

The trolley caught fire, its flames illuminating the street as people tumbled and bled on it. A woman five feet away cowered behind a palm tree, and Cyan shouted repeatedly at her to call an ambulance until the woman nodded and pulled out her cell phone.

Cyan took steps toward the trolley, the crushed cars. A dark blue Mercedes had taken the brunt of the trolley's wrath, so she was understandably shocked when the driver's side door opened, and a man in a tuxedo rolled out into the street. She hurried to pull him from the wreckage, wrapping her hands around his upper arm.

"Can you walk?" she shouted over the sound of moans and crackling fire.

Blood covered his face from what looked to be a head wound, and he said something.

"What?" Cyan leaned closer.

"Zoe." He pulled away from her to go back to the crushed car, the back of which glowed with orange flames from the trolley.

"Hey!" She tried to drag him backwards, but he had about six inches and eighty pounds on her slight frame. "You can't—"

He turned suddenly and took hold of Cyan's shoulders. "Help me," he said. "Help me get her out."

She would have nodded and moved a lot faster. She would have said something. She would have remembered to breathe if she didn't know his face so very well—the face she'd known since childhood, since the first time Sibyl's visions of Cyan's true love led to painting after painting after…

"Oh, my God," she gasped.

"Please," he begged.

She did nod, finally, and followed her destiny toward a burning mass of metal. He leaned in first, but somehow, they both fit through the door. Cyan winced when she saw the woman, dressed in a beautiful, black gown and covered in blood that resembled an oil slick. The man at Cyan's side didn't hesitate as he reached for her.

"The seat, it's…" He looked around. "Something's…"

The passenger side door was crushed in, as was the roof above. The woman was similarly crushed into her seat—all this as the flames moved closer. Sweat dripped from Cyan's forehead and into her eyes like tears.

"Let me get in the back," she said. Once there, she saw how the back of the passenger seat was bent forward. "I think I can pull backwards on the seat, and we can get her out." She looked up at his familiar face. "Okay?"

He nodded, taking firmer hold on the woman in evening dress.

Cyan wished she had her father's strength, her mother's magic. Instead, she had her skinny legs, which she planted against the door as she pulled on the passenger seat. She pulled until she thought her arms might give out, until she heard a sound like a sob escape the man's lips and he finally tugged the woman free, out of the car, into the street. The flames licked up the outside of the Mercedes; the windows glowed red.

Cyan tumbled out onto Broad Street beside the couple. Sirens grew louder, approaching, as the man in the tuxedo brushed blood-soaked hair from the woman's face. He kissed her forehead, her cheeks. "Zoe, wake up. Zoe."

Cyan watched him. It was *him*, wasn't it, her Dof? It would have been easier to tell if he hadn't been covered in his own blood, if his face hadn't been wrinkled in anguish over the limp form in his arms—if the only light hadn't been the dancing flames of a burning Charleston trolley.

He lifted the unconscious woman from the street and cradled her in his arms before looking up at Cyan. "Thank you." His eyes were red and wet. "Are you all right?"

With his beloved in his arms, why would he ask *her* such a thing?

"What's your name?" he asked, his hands caressing the cheeks of the unconscious woman.

"Cyan Burroughs."

He nodded. "I'm Liam. And this is Zoe."

The dancing lights of an ambulance replaced the fire beyond. "She's going to be okay," Cyan said, unsure if it was a lie. She wanted to reach out and touch his shoulder—give some kind of physical comfort—but didn't.

"Yeah," he said over the sound of rushing feet.

Then, there were paramedics pawing at them. Cyan pushed their hands away and stood, said she was fine. She stepped back and watched Liam, sitting near Zoe as they worked, even as his own head wound continued to paint his face red.

And then she ran.

Cyan ran away.

Liam watched her through glass as he talked quietly to the doctor in the hall. He'd never seen Zoe weak before, never seen her in a hospital bed, tied up to tubes and covered in bandages as the beeping machines measured how much life she had left.

"She suffered severe head trauma and lost a lot of blood. She's in a coma, Mr. Cody."

He wanted to hear her laugh. He wanted to twirl around the floor at her school fundraiser. He wanted to squeeze her body to his until she whispered his name.

"Mr. Cody?"

"Sorry." He looked away from his broken love. "What?"

"Is there any family you can call?"

"No, she doesn't…" He shook his head. "She doesn't have any family."

"What about you?"

"No." He ran his hand over the top of his head, through his hair, and winced when he hit the bandage on his forehead, stitches beneath. "Orphans, both of us."

"How about friends?" The female doctor smiled up at him, trying to be kind. "You should have friends around you right now."

He thought of the people from work: the restaurant owner, the chefs, the bartenders and waitresses. He wouldn't call them friends. "We only moved here three weeks ago. Her boss. I should call Zoe's boss. We were on our way to a fundraiser." He gestured with a shaking hand to his bloody tux. "Were a lot of people hurt tonight?"

The doctor nodded, hands in her white lab coat pockets. "Many. Some dead. In a way, you're lucky. Zoe still has a chance." She took steps away from him, back toward the ER downstairs. "Will you be staying the night?"

He stared at Zoe's limp body. "Yes."

"I'll have a cot brought up."

"No." He shook his head. "I won't sleep."

At the sound of the doctor's retreating footsteps, Liam entered Zoe's room. The place smelled of gauze and disinfectant. He pulled a cushioned chair close to her bedside, sat, and folded his hands in his lap. He watched the machines record her heartbeat and breathing.

He needed to call her boss, her school. Surely, by then, news of the tragedy on Broad Street had reached the Brighton School fundraiser, and perhaps, people were wondering why Zoe wasn't there, maybe knowing she lived below Broad. Maybe already suspecting the worst.

Yes, he needed to call her boss, but first, he stood and took her cold hand in his. "You're supposed to talk to people in comas," he whispered. "Or at least I think I saw that on a TV show, like you're supposed to be able to hear me or something. Can you hear me, Zoe?"

The machines chirped.

"I had something in mind for tonight. See, I've been carrying this ring." He laid his palm over his suit coat pocket. "I bought it in Charleston, actually. I was walking up East Bay and saw it in the front window of a jewelry store. You're going to say it's too much, but I saw it and knew I wanted to marry you. I want to marry you, Zoe, so you can't do this stupid thing. You can't lay here like this. You have to wake up. You have to wake—"

"Mr. Cody?"

He closed his eyes against the voice at the door.

"Mr. Cody, you have a phone call."

He glanced over his shoulder to find a young woman in purple scrubs.

"It should ring through." She nodded to the plastic phone on the table by Zoe's bed, which made Liam realize he had no idea where his phone was or Zoe's. Probably still in their burning car.

"Thank you."

Even though he was expecting it, he still jumped when the phone rang.

"Hello."

"Liam?" It was the owner of the Bistro, Max. He sounded just this side of hysterical.

"Yeah. Is everyone okay down there?"

Max let out a long, loud breath. "It's a damn mess. Horrible. We closed the restaurant, of course. Then, once things calmed down a bit, I saw your burnt-up car and called the hospital, and they said Zoe was there."

"She's in a coma. Her side took the brunt of it. Do they know what happened?"

"They're saying something about the trolley."

Liam remembered driving slowly down Broad in the midst of Charleston rush hour and playing some stupid country music to annoy Zoe. He remembered seeing the trolley in front of them, then—

"I think there was an explosion," Liam said. "I think I saw a flash of red."

Max let out another loud sigh. "Let's not worry about that right now. You worry about Zoe. What's the doctor say?"

"She's in a coma. They don't know anything—don't know if she'll wake up today or a year from now or never."

"She'll wake up, Liam. She's got you to come home to."

His eyes burned a bit at that.

"Do you need anything?" Max asked.

He paused. "I need Zoe back."

Chapter Three

Cyan sat on the cold stone of Grandmother Plainacher's grave in the Church of St. Agnes cemetery. Usually, she talked to her grandmother, asked her about their family, about the Craft, but she had nothing to say that night, no questions. She reached into her wallet and pulled out the folded, hand-drawn picture of her destined true love. She stared at him for a while and then stood.

It was easy to walk right into Charleston Memorial Hospital undeterred. The first floor was in chaos, patients still pouring in from the accident on Broad Street—the accident Cyan knew was no accident at all. There had been a witch present, and he had done something awful.

The more she thought back to the bloody scene on Broad, the more she wondered if she'd just imagined Liam. Maybe Sybil's paintings had wormed into her brain. Maybe every man in need of saving would look like Cyan's "Dof," her invisible man. Except if what she thought she saw amidst the flames was true, he wasn't invisible. He was real, and he was early.

It would take some work to find Liam and Zoe since she didn't have last names. It would take even more work to look him in the face. She walked up to administration where a harried nurse shifted papers, eyes wide and afraid. "Excuse me," Cyan said. "I'm looking for my friends, Liam and Zoe."

"Last name?" the nurse barked.

"Uh—"

A soft hand fell on Cyan's shoulder. "Did you say you're a friend of Mr. Cody's?"

Liam *Cody*. Sure. Cyan nodded, and the female doctor smiled.

"Good. He needs a friend right now. I'll take you up."

Cyan followed closely behind, surrounded by the sounds of groaning and the hurried movements of doctors trying to save lives. She didn't even know if Mr. Cody was Liam, but she followed nonetheless. What choice did she have?

After a quick elevator ride, the doctor walked down the quiet hallway of the ICU. When she stopped in front of one room, Cyan recognized the beautiful woman in bed with a tube down her throat and Liam's black tuxedo coat.

"Thank you," she whispered to the helpful doctor, who nodded and went back to work.

It was hard to hide the sound of combat boots, so Liam turned when she entered the room. He had a bandage on his head, and the collar of his white dress shirt was open and stained red. He tilted his head and stood, staring at her.

"It's good to see you," he said, his mouth turning up on the edges.

Cyan played with one of her blonde braids. "You sure about that?"

He nodded. "My hero. I don't remember your name."

"Cyan."

He reached his hand out to her. She moved to shake, but they both paused when they saw dried blood on her palms.

"I'm sorry." She crossed her arms under her leather jacket.

"There's a bathroom." He pointed to the door in the corner of the room.

Cyan hid behind that door, scrubbing her hands, and stared into her own gray eyes in the mirror to make sure she wasn't wearing blood anywhere else. When she stepped back into the gauze-smelling hospital room, Liam hadn't moved from where he stood.

Cyan stayed near the door. "I didn't mean to impose. I just wanted to see if she was all right."

Liam glanced back at the bed. "She's not. I mean, she's not yet. She will be."

Cyan gestured to his bandage. "Your head."

"My hairline will never be the same. And the dry-cleaning bill is going to be a nightmare."

He said it all with such a deadpan expression, Cyan almost didn't realize he was joking. When she did, she snorted and covered her face. He chuckled once, quickly, and that moment of levity was enough to convince Cyan: this was the man from her aunt's visions.

Her eyes brushed over his short, dark brown hair. Beyond a few cuts near his eye and across his forehead, he had the flawless complexion of Sybil's paintings. He looked like a man who never had to shave—or perhaps shaved every morning, with a deadly sharp straight razor, so smooth was his skin. He had big, bright eyes, maybe green or hazel; she couldn't tell in the dim, hospital room lights. Cyan hadn't expected him to be so big, possibly because Sybil had never painted much more than Liam's face. She felt like an elf next to him.

She looked at the floor. "I'm sorry, I'm staring at you."

"I've seen you before," he said. "You work on Broad Street."

"Yeah. My aunt owns Sea Books."

"I'm the manager at Broad Street Bistro."

"Oh." He'd been a block away from her, but for how long? "You're not from here. You talk funny."

He feigned offense. "I talk funny? Where do you crazy southerners get off saying I talk funny?" He sighed. "I grew up in Ireland. Most days, I think the accent's gone."

"It's not," she said. "Have you been here long?"

"America or Charleston?"

"Charleston."

"Only about three weeks."

It was a strange relief to know he hadn't been a block away from her for months, years. "Are you and Zoe married?"

Apparently, that was the exact wrong thing to say. The tall, strong man in a destroyed suit covered his face. His shoulders shook with sudden, silent sobs. Cyan rarely touched people and never comforted, yet what had she told her mother just earlier that day? What would she do when she met her Dof?

Keep him safe.

Cyan got closer and put her small hands on his arms. There wasn't an electric shock, no nod from the great beyond of their fated meeting. The suit fabric felt cold against her palms, but she could feel him shaking—his whole body, shaking.

"I'm sorry," she whispered.

He hugged her, and despite his size, he felt small in her arms. Cyan had never hugged a man before, except her father, but she didn't need to be guided into an embrace. Liam clung to her, so she clung back. Her face pressed against his chest, and he smelled like smoke and the remnants of men's cologne.

"I'm sorry," she said again and felt his hand at the base of her neck, his fingers in her hair as he held her tighter, tighter. She looked to the broken body on the bed and said, "She'll wake up. She'll wake up."

She kept saying it until he was too exhausted to stand and she led him to his chair by Zoe's bed. Cyan sat on the floor in the corner and watched the clock tick.

Liam woke with a pain that extended up the side of his neck and directly into his temple. He reached his hand up to poke at the pain only to have his finger encounter a thick, white bandage, which was when he noticed the beeping sounds, the smell of antiseptic, and remembered where he was.

His eyes popped open to early morning light, tilting its way pathetically through the thick, hospital blinds. He sat in a thinly cushioned chair, legs extended in front of him. Zoe hadn't moved an inch in her pale, white hospital bed—which her skin was beginning to mimic in the places where it wasn't a shade of purple, yellow, or dark brown. Bruises. She had bruises everywhere he could see, and the tube down her throat looked like some sadistic pacifier between her lips.

He rubbed his eyes and then heard a noise from the floor beneath the window: a sort of sighing moan. His eyes darted down.

A woman slept, curled in a little ball against the wall. She used her black leather coat as a pillow, and her long, thick, braided hair fell over her cheeks and cascaded down her neck. Her name was Cyan, he remembered, although now, looking at her in the morning light, he knew her as something else, too: Blondie. It was what some of the boys at the Bistro called her, and she'd almost knocked Liam over the day before. Her good looks were legend at the restaurant, although she didn't much resemble the cartoon character or the 80s rock star. Her look was too wild for the comic book girl, and she was too small to be Debbie Harry. He remembered the color of her eyes: a shade of blue that had all the color washed away, to more of a deep, dark gray. She smelled like spice and smoke but not cigarettes. He remembered all that, but he couldn't remember falling asleep or apparently giving Cyan no other option than to sleep on the floor like an unwelcome housecat.

Liam stood and kissed Zoe on the forehead but pulled back quickly when he found her skin cold. He wanted to pick her up and hold her to his chest, warm her, but all the beeping machines and IVs made that impossible.

He leaned down next to Cyan, put his hand on her shoulder, and said her name.

She startled and looked up at him.

"Hey," he said. "You didn't have to stay."

"Oh, I…" She pushed herself up on one elbow. A heavy, black and white amulet hung around her neck. "I was tired." She sat up and stayed on the floor, legs curled beneath her. "What time is it?"

He sat on the floor, too. "I have no idea."

He watched her search around in her jean pockets, then jacket, before pulling out a black cell phone. "Oh, shit, I have like sixty messages from my family." She stood suddenly, as did Liam, who then almost fell over. With lightning speed, Cyan's hand reached out and held him by the forearm. Her grip was like iron. "You okay?"

"Will be, once the room stops spinning."

She expelled an irritated gasp and dragged him back to the chair by Zoe's bed. "You have a head injury. Where the fuck is the nurse?" Meanwhile, she pounded away at her cell phone, one hand still on his arm.

"I'm fine."

"You need to go home. In the sunlight, you look like an extra in a slasher flick."

He chuckled weakly. "I don't want to leave her alone."

"You said you work at the Bistro. Can someone from there sit with her while you go home and wash up? And when did you eat last?"

He looked up to find her studying his face, her full lips set in a thin line. "I don't know."

She glanced away from him and toward Zoe, motionless on the bed. "You shouldn't eat hospital food. I mean, no one should eat hospital food. Maybe…" Cyan seemed to be wrestling with something. "Maybe I can bring you something to eat."

Her hand was still wrapped around his wrist, and he suspected she didn't even notice. "You've done enough. You don't even know me."

Her laugh sounded frantic. He thought it would have been a pretty thing if not for the panic in her eyes.

"You don't know me, Cyan. Do you?"

She pulled her hand away from him. "Why would you ask something like that?" She took a breath in through her nose. "That sounded a lot angrier than I meant it to."

"Well, you did just wake up on a floor. Gives new meaning to wrong side of the bed."

"You need to go home, Liam." She tapped some more on her cell phone, not looking at him.

He looked at Zoe. "I'll call someone from work."

"I need to go."

He rested his elbows on his knees and leaned forward. "Yeah, of course."

Cyan didn't move to leave. She didn't move at all. When he looked up, she stared at him, top teeth nibbling her bottom lip.

"What?" he asked.

She reached out and ran her fingers through his hair, then her whole hand over the top of his head. She pulled back as though she'd been zapped. "Jesus, I'm sorry. That was weird."

"No, it felt good actually. My head aches."

She stared at him again until he felt like he was being studied, a man-sized bug under an invisible microscope.

"Do you have any… I mean…" She tugged on her braids, and her eyes darted around the room. "There's got to be paper around here."

There was a little pad with the name of some drug at the bottom in purple letters. Cyan scrawled something across the paper's surface, violently, as if she was actually angry at the paper and then handed the pad to Liam.

"That's my number," she said. "You don't have to use it, but if you need anything."

He stood and held the paper in his hand. The top of her head came up to his chin. "Thank you. For everything."

"Go home, Liam."

He nodded as Cyan said a quick goodbye. He turned to watch her long hair dance across her back as she walked, or more like ran, back into the hospital hallway. She seemed to be in quite a rush to get away from him.

Chapter Four

Cyan texted everyone—Sybil, her mom and dad—and told them to meet at Sea Books… after she told them, obviously, that she was alive. Still, as she left the hospital, she knew she was in for it. After the massive accident on Broad Street and then silence from Cyan, she was certain her family had spent the entire night calling the police and then, the hospital, looking for her dead body. Good thing conjuring spells didn't affect her, protected from magical detection by Grandmother Plainacher's black agate necklace, or who knew what spells her mother would have done to try and summon her back to them?

The morning was dreadfully cold and damp as she passed still-flowering gardens that hid the huge plantation homes set back from the road. Above her, the sky was the color of a murky pond; a storm approached. She almost tripped over crooked sidewalks as she thought back to the hospital scene and touching Liam's hair.

What the hell was that about?

Cyan hadn't planned to caress the man's head, it just sort of happened. One second, she was staring down at the face she'd been staring at all her life—through pictures. The next second, her hand just moved, fingers running through soft hair. Still, no glow of magic light, but touching him had indeed made something glow inside her. She wanted to touch him more, a sensation she'd never had before, so focused was she on learning the Craft and preparing for the War.

Now, as she walked, she thought more about the way he made her feel: warm, nervous, and sort of dizzy. Liam was better looking in person than in Sybil's paintings, maybe because of the way he moved, the way his eyes crinkled, the way…

Cyan shook her head when she turned onto Broad Street, annoyed at her own distraction. Up ahead, the street was blocked. A palm tree had fallen over in the chaos. Remnants of burnt cars—Liam's included—still remained, although crews looked to be working hard to at least sweep up the rubble. Cops were everywhere, trying to figure out how this happened. Cyan knew, but she wasn't going to the authorities. She was going to her family.

As soon as she stepped into Sea Books, the room erupted in high-pitched, female shouting, mostly from Rue, who even used Cyan's real first name—that of a woman burned in 415 AD for witchcraft. What kind of name legacy was that anyway?

"Where have you been, Hypatia?"

She brushed past her mother and hoped someone had made tea. "Mother, I hate that name."

"Well, it's yours, and I'm about one more smart ass comment away from setting up a stake for you in the middle of Broad!"

"Rue." The sound of Cyan's father's voice soothed the whole room—even Sybil, who stood in the corner, wringing her red hair. "Why don't we all just calm down now? Cyan is safe." Drake Burroughs guided his beautiful, hysterical wife to an overstuffed, paisley chair in the corner and stood in front of Cyan. He was a giant of a man with dark blue eyes and perpetual five o'clock shadow. "Why don't you tell us where you've been, honey?"

"Sybil, you might want to sit down."

Her aunt did as instructed, pulling up another ugly chair from the recesses of bookshelves.

"I was on Broad last night. When it happened."

Rue exhaled loudly and put her hand to her forehead. "I knew it."

"Mother, I'm fine." She looked up at Drake. "But Daddy, before the accident, I saw someone. I saw a witch."

Drake put his massive hands on his hips. "You're sayin' a witch caused the accident."

"Yes. I tried to…" She shook her head. "I shouted, but it was too late. I saw a red light, and the trolley went flying through the air."

"That's a damn strong witch," he said.

"Yeah. You thinking what I'm thinking?"

"Dorcha," her father whispered.

Rue sprung to her feet. "Here? Now? But Cyan still doesn't have any powers. How can she fight back without any powers?"

"Yes, Mother, I know, but maybe they'll start manifesting now that he's made an appearance. Maybe me seeing him last night will push things along."

Drake put one of his hands on Cyan's shoulder. "Do you feel any different?"

She thought of Liam. "Well. There's something else. The trolley caused a lot of damage, but one of the cars was practically crushed. The driver got out, but his girlfriend was trapped, so we worked together to get her free." She paused. "It was dark, and there was fire. I wasn't sure."

"Sure of what, dear?" Sybil stood and crept up behind her.

"My Dof. The driver was my Dof."

Sybil gasped, and her mother's forehead crinkled. "Your true love," she said.

"But I wasn't sure, so I went to the hospital to see him not covered in blood." She cleared her throat. "And it's him. Definitely. I spent the night at the hospital. That's where I've been."

"You slept with a stranger!" Rue screeched.

"Mother! No, not like that. Shit, I slept on the floor. I just… he seemed so broken. His girlfriend is in a coma, and no one knows if she's going to wake up. They're new to Charleston, so he doesn't have anyone. I was just trying to…" She brushed braids from her face. "I don't know what the fuck I was doing there." She melted into Rue's now abandoned chair.

"Language, young lady."

"Rue." Drake put his hand on his wife's arm and knelt in front of Cyan. "Did anything out of the ordinary happen when you were with him?"

"Like, magical? No." She pointed at Sybil. "And it would be really messed up if destiny makes his girlfriend die just so I can be with my so-called true love."

Sybil's freckles twitched. "I don't think that's quite how it works, dear."

"It better not."

"I want to see him," Rue growled.

"Mother, you are not busting into that hospital room."

"I don't have to. Sybil." Rue waved toward the secret back room of Sea Books, and Sybil moved quickly.

"What's his name?" Drake asked.

"Liam. He has a funny accent."

Sybil came back with a small bowl and a mirror the size of her head—the Plainacher family scrying mirror.

Cyan stomped between Rue and her supplies. "What, you're going to spy on him? What if he's picking his nose?"

"Everyone picks their nose, dear," Sybil said as she set the dark chrome mirror near the bookshop point of sales. She then hurried to make sure the front door was locked as Rue carried the small bowl around the store, picking sprigs of herb while whispering incantations in Gaelic.

Cyan stared into the black center of the mirror that reflected nothing unless a witch made it so—unless a witch directly requested to see a particular person. She pursed her lips at her father.

"She just wants to see him, little one." He kissed her forehead.

"It feels so invasive."

"It is, but so is your mama."

Rue set the bowl of herbs before the scrying mirror. She rolled up the sleeves of her blue linen shirt and took a deep breath before waving her hands over the bowl. Her palms glowed a bright, clean white. "His name, Hypatia."

When she didn't speak, her dad nudged her in the back.

Cyan sighed. "Liam Cody."

Rue whispered some more, eyes closed. Sybil stood behind her sister and put one hand on her shoulder, her own palm emitting a light pink glow. Then, they whispered together. Cyan recognized the words. Her extensive studies had taught her how to use a scrying mirror; she'd just never had the power to do so. There was the occasional muttering of Liam's name amidst the incantations, and then, the mirror began to change. It shifted from depthless ebony into a haze of warm light and some movement. The image continued to clear until a tidy bedroom revealed itself... and Liam in nothing but a towel around his waist.

Cyan squeaked. "Mother! Turn it off!"

"Oh, my," Rue said.

"Indeed," Sybil agreed, moving closer to the mirror.

Cyan shoved between her family and the scrying mirror, her back to Liam's semi-naked, incredibly attractive body. "He just got out of the shower."

"What do you think?" Rue asked. "Runner or yoga?"

Together, the sisters agreed, "Runner."

"Daddy, is he..." Cyan tilted her head back toward the mirror.

Drake dared a glance over his daughter's shoulder. "Yes, he's decent."

Rue shoved Cyan out of the way, and both she and Sybil studied Liam as he walked slowly around his and Zoe's apartment, wearing dark jeans and a black button-down. Cyan tried not to watch this massive invasion of Liam's privacy, but she caught a few glimpses of the condo the couple was trying to make feel like home with pictures of San Francisco, still-packed boxes, and a blank big screen TV.

"It's really him," Sybil said.

"I know."

Rue was silent.

"Mother?"

Rue watched the man in the mirror. "Is his head all right?"

Cyan could just barely see the gash in his forehead, pulled together by stitches. "Yeah. His girlfriend got the worst of it."

"And she's in a coma?" Rue asked.

"Yes."

Rue shrugged. "People wake from comas."

Cyan looked up at her giant of a father, who watched his wife with concern. "Mother. Why are you upset?"

Rue said a string of unintelligible words, and the scrying mirror turned black. "Did you touch him when you were together?"

Cyan hesitated, and then nodded.

"And nothing magic happened? You didn't feel anything?"

Cyan looked at her feet, anywhere but at her father. "Well, I felt *something*."

Sybil giggled until Rue glared her way. "This boy, this Liam you've been drawing my daughter's whole life, you're sure they're meant to be together. Then, why does he already have a woman?"

"Well." Sybil fidgeted with a hand-woven scarf on a nearby rack. "He's meant to be Cyan's true love. It doesn't mean they'll be together."

"What?" Cyan hissed.

"I'm sorry if I wasn't clear on that."

"You're saying that I'm destined to fall in love with him, but he might never fall in love with me."

Sybil looked up through strings of red hair. "Oh, he'll fall in love with you, girl, but that doesn't promise you'll end up together. People in love hurt each other every day. It's not always happily ever after."

Cyan looked to her daddy, who looked at her mother, who looked at Sybil.

"But, I don't know," Sybil shouted. "It could all end up just fine. You could have a dozen babies with that beautiful piece of man."

Cyan thought of Zoe. "Not if the cost is a woman's life."

"I see what I see," Sybil said, "and I see him. Always have. And when I see him, I see him with you."

Cyan growled. "I can't think about this right now. What about the witch I saw in the street? He was obviously going after someone in the trolley."

Drake nodded. "We need to figure out who was on that trolley."

He did go home, like Cyan said, but he couldn't stand to stay there—not with all the reminders of Zoe from twenty-four hours ago, before the trolley flipped, before the coma. Her perfume bottle was still on the sink, cap off. His glass of wine still sat next to it, half finished. He rushed back to the hospital.

The nurse checked Liam's injuries while he lurked about in Zoe's room, living on coffee and grief. Although the cut on his head was deep, she said it was nothing to worry about. He mentioned the headaches, and she said, sure, that could happen. He didn't tell her he'd been having headaches long before the car accident.

A sudden storm rose up outside, pummeling the hospital windows like tiny fingers tapping, tapping, desperate to come inside. He stared at Zoe's unmoving body and considered buying earplugs, only to silence the storm and the constant beeping of machines. The sound was almost as painful as the stitched up wound on his head and the bruises on his ribs.

"Liam."

He looked over his shoulder at the sound of his name and saw his boss from the Bistro. Liam rose to greet him. "You didn't have to come, Max."

Max shook his head but not in disagreement—more in disbelief that Liam would doubt his visit. "The whole restaurant won't stop asking questions about you."

Liam nodded and allowed himself to be hugged. Max Henny was definitely a hugger, even though he more closely resembled a high-priced lawyer than a Care Bear. He was almost as tall as Liam, trim and thin with a shiny, hairless head and impeccable clothes—usually perfectly pressed black suits—although he never wore a tie. Max had built the Broad Street Bistro from the ground up, and even though he was now filthy rich, he still worked almost every night and took a personal interest in all his employees.

They'd gotten along well at Liam's interview, and, after a quick check of Liam's references, Max offered him the job. He started working the next day since the Bistro was desperate, what with Liam's predecessor having quit quite suddenly due to heart health issues. They needed Liam as much as he needed the job.

Max pulled out of their embrace and looked at Zoe. "How is she?"

"No change so far, but they keep telling me it's only been a day so it's too early to tell."

"Don't worry," Max said forcefully. "She'll be fine."

"Yeah."

Max turned and held tight to Liam's shoulders. "What happened to your head?"

"It's nothing. I think I just hit the steering wheel. A couple stitches."

"Do you feel strange at all? Head injuries can have lasting effects."

"I'm okay." He shrugged Max's hands off his upper arms. Liam had never had a father, so the extra care was sometimes appreciated—but, right then, it felt suffocating. "Have they figured anything out about the accident?"

Max put his hands on his hips and took a few steps toward the window, where the heavy rain now poured like one constant ocean wave down the glass. "You should see it today—glass everywhere, debris. They've been searching for evidence. I guess, like you said, for an explosion. I suppose the rain will wash that all away. Have the police talked to you?"

"Briefly." Liam hardly remembered the call from an hour ago. "Just on the phone. I told them I saw a red flash."

"And you're sure that's all you saw?"

Liam shrugged. "What else was there to see? A red flash, and then, a flying trolley. Zoe didn't even scream. There wasn't time." He paused. "This is going to sound completely idiotic in South Carolina, but have any terrorist groups claimed responsibility?"

Max glanced back at him, a slight tilt to his lips.

"I know it's stupid. I'm just trying to figure out who would bomb a trolley." He sat back down in the chair by Zoe's bed.

"Well, the world today, who knows?" Max nodded. "Flowers got here fast."

The room was covered in bouquets from Zoe's co-workers and a couple from staff members at the Bistro—mostly from female employees Liam knew were attracted to him. Those bouquets were almost like sick jokes, screaming, *If she dies, I'm available.*

"I'd heard of Southern hospitality," Liam said. "Now I've seen it."

"I brought you this instead." Max pulled a silver flask from his inside suit pocket and handed it to Liam. "I know it's not a French Bordeaux, but I didn't think I could sneak a whole wine bottle in here."

Liam unscrewed the top and gave it a sniff. He may have been a wine specialist, but he recognized a nice scotch when he smelled it. He took a sip, no matter it was only noon. "Thank you." He took another sip and lifted the flask to Zoe in a one-sided salute. "I can't imagine we just moved here for her to die, Max."

"She's not going to die."

"How do you know?"

"You'll save her."

Liam smirked. "I'm no doctor."

"She knows you're here. She's not going anywhere, okay?" Max put his hand on Liam's shoulder and squeezed. "Call me if you need anything."

"I don't have your number anymore. My cell phone was in the car. Probably burnt to ash by now."

"I'll write it down." Max circled Liam's chair and reached for a piece of paper on the table by Zoe's bed. "Who's Cyan Burroughs?"

Liam didn't move his eyes from the love of his life. "The girl who helped save Zoe. And me, I guess." He took another sip of scotch. "Everyone at the Bistro calls her Blondie."

Max scoffed. "That tiny thing dragged you from a car?"

"She's apparently a lot stronger than she looks."

"Some people say she comes from a family of witches. Maybe she used her magic powers."

Liam chuckled. "You guys believe in that stuff around here?"

While writing, Max said, "Her aunt owns a bookstore right down from the Bistro. Maybe I'll drop in and tell her thanks."

"It's all right, Max. I don't think she'd appreciate the praise. She seems pretty private, really."

"Wouldn't you be, if you were a witch?" Max returned the piece of paper to the table.

"There's no such thing as witches, but I appreciate the distracting dialogue."

Max gave his shoulder another squeeze. "Anything you need, call, even if it's a rare steak from the Bistro. Tommy will run it up. We've got you covered at work. We're a family at the Bistro."

Liam nodded and strangely wanted to call Cyan.

Chapter Five

Pearlz Restaurant was loud, crowded, and smelled of fresh oysters. Cyan sat at the bar where she awaited her own dozen raw blue points. Her Bloody Mary rested on a small, white napkin in front of her, sweating as ice melted. She took a sip, and thanks to Pearlz's in-house, spicy vodka, smiled a little at the burn she loved so much. Cyan wasn't an overly smiley person, but oysters and Bloody Mary's often did the trick.

She waited for her father.

Once they realized they needed to assign an identity to the trolley target, Drake was sent forth to do one of his tricks. He didn't exactly become invisible, but he had a magical way of shielding himself from the sight of others, like a ghost you only see out the corner of your eye. He could sneak into anywhere like that, even the Charleston Police Department, even the hospital—although she'd made her father swear to go nowhere near Liam or Zoe. He went in search of records, names, anything that might enlighten them as to why a dark witch flipped a trolley in the middle of Broad Street and killed people.

She thought of Zoe. For all Cyan knew, the woman was awake, and Liam was happy and everything was all right—for them. She thought Liam might call her if Zoe died. She hoped he would. She pulled the folded drawing of him from her wallet and looked at the black and white scrawling by her crazy aunt. One thing could be said for Sybil: she was an amazing artist. The resemblance between the picture and the real man was astounding, although it was nice to see him in color. Cyan finally knew the ashy dark brown of his hair, the bright green of his eyes, and the cream with a dash of coffee complexion. She knew the way he moved, like a purebred horse, really—the grace and balance of a career showman. To have landed the job as manager at the Broad Street Bistro, Liam had to be a man of appearances and charm. He looked the part; he talked the part. He was nothing like her.

She felt her father's presence before she saw him and hurriedly returned the picture of Liam to her wallet. Drake seemed to materialize beside her just as her tray of oysters appeared.

"Shit," she gasped. "Daddy, I hate when you do that."

He smiled at her with his big teeth—Drake Burroughs was big everywhere—and took a seat with a stack of paper in his huge hands. Familiar with the family, the bartender brought over a Coast IPA and placed it in front of Cyan's father.

"Did you get what we needed?" She squeezed a lemon over the slimy creatures in their silver shells.

"Do I ever disappoint?" He tugged a piece of her hair, which made her glare. "A full list of everyone on the trolley at the time of the attack and the names of who lived, who died."

"Do you recognize any of the names?"

"Nothing I noticed. No ancient Craft family names, no." He took a Drake-sized sip of beer, which was a normal man's gulp. "Most of the victims were tourists."

"Okay." She poured a salty oyster into her mouth, using its shell as a serving spoon. "Maybe we should only focus on the people who *aren't* tourists?"

"Why do you say that?"

"It's possible the witch who did this traveled to get his victim, followed him or her here, but why attack someone on their vacation?"

Drake frowned. "People put their guard down on vacation."

"So maybe we *only* look at tourists?"

"I think we look at everyone on this list. We also have to consider that if the dark witch was successful in his attack, if his intended target is indeed dead, then he's probably long gone."

She added some Tabasco and swallowed another treat. "And therefore not our problem."

"Well…" Drake lifted one shoulder.

"What?"

"The power it takes to flip a trolley? That's a lot of power, little girl."

Cyan shook her Bloody Mary glass until the ice danced. "I know you think it could be the Dorcha. So isn't there, like, a database of people with one blue eye and one green?"

"You're referring to the *Book of Shadows* prophecy."

"Yes." She slapped the heavy wooden bar in irritation. "The only clue we have about the Dorcha: they will have one green eye and one blue eye—and their lifetime will coincide with mine as Loach."

Drake shook his head. "There isn't a database, no, but be sure to look closely at people's eyes, huh?" He paused. "Then again, a powerful witch aware of the prophecy would cast their eyes to match."

"Yeah, fucking fantastic. Daddy, if whoever caused the accident was the Dorcha, why aren't I shooting lightning out of my fingers yet?"

He chuckled. "It might not start immediately, and it could start small. When you reach for a spoon, maybe it shakes before you touch it. Maybe try some incantations and see if anything happens."

She ate another oyster. "I'm done talking about this right now."

"I know you're frustrated by your lack of ability, but it'll come."

"Yeah, great, just in time for me to have to kill someone."

"You were born with a destiny—"

"Daddy, please, can I just eat my oysters, get a good night sleep, and I'll dig into these names tomorrow morning?"

Her father nodded and gestured for another beer. "Sure, honey."

Except, after finishing her oysters, Cyan didn't go home. The rain having finally stopped for the day, she started walking—her apartment was only about thirty feet away—and kept walking. She mulled over the attack on the trolley, what she'd actually seen, which had been very little before the blast of red light. She considered, briefly, what it might mean if the War had just begun and even wondered what it would feel like to finally hone the Craft like the rest of her family. By the time she was done thinking, she was standing outside Charleston Memorial Hospital.

She wasn't invisible like her father, but she was sneaky. Years of self-defense training had taught her how to be quiet, so it was really no problem at all getting past the front desk and up to the second floor.

The doorway to Zoe's room was partially open, and Cyan heard the sound of plastic hitting plastic from inside. When she stuck her head in the doorway, she found Zoe, still unconscious, and Liam, dropping little circles into a Connect Four.

"That game's a lot more interesting if you play it with someone else."

He turned and stood at the sound of her voice. "Probably. I was just spelling out letters of the alphabet." He gestured to the letter L in black, surrounded by red, down the center of the board. "They have a whole room of games. I guess for kids that get sick."

Cyan leaned against the doorframe.

Liam stood with his hands in his pockets.

"I don't know why I'm here," she said. "I meant to walk home."

"You knew I needed an adversary for Connect Four?"

She rolled her eyes toward the ceiling and smirked.

"I'm glad you came. I, um…" He glanced toward the bed, and then pressed his lips together in an extremely tight smile. "Her silence. It's weird. Zoe was never very quiet."

Cyan pulled a second chair beside Liam's and sat. She pushed the little button at the bottom of the Connect Four board. The plastic circles bounced into the cardboard box below, and Cyan picked up a black one, dropped it into the bottom of the center row.

Liam sat next to her and put a red circle in the far right row. Cyan added a black one to the right of her original. Liam added a red one to the top of his. Cyan added a black to the left of her original. Liam added another red to the row on the right. Cyan dropped a final black one.

"I win."

"What?" He studied the board.

"It's the oldest trick in the book." She crossed her arms over her chest and leaned back in the uncomfortable hospital chair.

"Devious."

"Simple."

He leaned back, too, eyes still on the game.

"Why haven't they brought you a cot?" She didn't even ask if he planned to go home to sleep, as she knew the answer.

"I guess they forgot. After the accident, I don't think a healthy guy needing sleep is a priority."

"Sleep's overrated anyway."

His brow furrowed. "I completely disagree."

"It's eight hours that could be used in a much more fruitful manner."

"It's eight hours of bliss." He turned sideways in his chair to face her. The dim bedside lamp lit his lips. "I once took a three hour nap. It was one of the best days of my life."

She chuckled.

"So how do you use the hours spent not sleeping?"

"Reading. Walking. Charleston's a very good walking city. I like the cemeteries. My grandmother is buried in one on Meeting Street, behind St. Agnes. I visit her sometimes."

"Your family is from here?"

"Pretty much." She paused. "You don't think it's weird that I like cemeteries?"

He tapped his fingers on the arm of the chair. "Probably good places to catch a nap."

She yawned despite herself.

He reciprocated.

"You can't sleep in a chair again," she said.

"And you can't sleep on the floor."

"I'm getting you a cot." She stood, but before she started walking to the door, his hand wrapped around her wrist. Cyan looked down at him to find his eyes on Zoe.

"Do you think she can hear us?" he said. "Do you think she knows I'm here?"

Cyan knelt at the side of his chair. His grip on her wrist loosened until their fingers melted together, hand over hand. There was no spark of the Craft with this man, no, but Cyan certainly felt her cheeks warm at the innocent intimacy of the gesture. "I think she can feel you, yeah."

"I'd like to hold her hand, but she's so cold. It freaks me out."

Cyan begrudgingly let go of Liam's hand and faced Zoe. She reached down and picked up the unconscious woman's limp hand—which was really quite cold, in fact—and held that cold hand between her own. "Come here," she told Liam, and she then rubbed Zoe's hand between hers until a semblance of warmth trickled into the tips of Zoe's fingers. "Hold her hand now."

Liam took Zoe's hand, warmed by Cyan's body heat. He sat on the edge of the hospital bed. "Zoe. It's Liam. Wake up, huh?"

Cyan turned her back on them, her eyes stinging with an emotion she couldn't identify. She'd said she would get him a cot; she was getting him a damn cot. But when she reached the door, he said her name, and she stopped.

"Why are you so kind to me?" he asked.

"You seem like a man who deserves kindness."

"Have we met before? Some other time, other place. You're so familiar."

"No," she said quickly and left the room. She didn't think about the folded picture of him in her wallet as she tracked down a nurse and found Liam a cot. She certainly didn't think about him as she hid beneath the covers of her bed at home. She dreamt of a flash of red light.

Chapter Six

The next morning, it wasn't a friend or work colleague who kicked him out of Zoe's room; it was her doctor. "You need to get some air," she told him.

Liam couldn't bear the thought of going back to their quiet condo alone, but he did go, long enough to throw on jogging pants, a t-shirt, and tennis shoes. Due to the scalded remnants of his cell phone, he had no music, but he decided he would make a stop at the Apple store on King following his run and pick up a new phone.

But what if something happened to Zoe? What if they couldn't reach him?

He changed his mind halfway into his usual five-mile jaunt and swung into the store to get a new phone. Standing outside, sweating, he called the hospital and left his number with the receptionist. Then, he took off again, at a speed he didn't usually utilize unless racing. Yet, he didn't race toward the finish line; he felt like he was running away not toward.

He turned the corner onto Broad and, mind half at the hospital, ran into someone. He was prepared to profusely apologize, but whomever he ran into grabbed his arm, twisted, and hurled him onto his chest on the pavement. His bruised ribs exploded in pain. His face, unfortunately, also caught a bit of concrete and he thought, fleetingly, *What amazing injuries I'm acquiring this week.* He felt a knee in the center of his back as he gasped for air. Sheets of paper peppered the sidewalk.

"Liam?"

He heard Cyan's voice but couldn't respond, the wind knocked entirely from his lungs.

She stopped kneeling on him at least. "Shit, I'm sorry."

He rolled onto his back, choking. His face felt wet but not with sweat—with something thicker.

"Your nose is bleeding." She said it as though angry at him. She knelt by his side and guided him to sitting before collecting the dropped pieces of paper surrounding them. "Come on." She dragged Liam to standing with strength he never expected her to have and pulled him down the sidewalk by his arm.

"I'm sorry," he muttered. "I'm sorry I ran into you."

"I'm sorry I just kicked your ass." She hugged the papers to her chest while continuing to pull him along. "You surprised me."

"Where'd you learn how to do that?"

"It's a hobby." She dragged him across the street and into a shop—a bookshop. The interior was lit by gold, glowing lanterns. Several pieces of aged but homey furniture sat between shelves. The place smelled of incense, reminiscent of Liam's "experimental" days back in California.

He used his shirt to wipe his nose and found his shirt stained bright red. Cyan, meanwhile, put down her messy stack of papers—some of them looked like hospital forms—and told him to sit.

"Cyan, I'm covered in sweat."

Lips pressed tightly together, she forced him into a cushioned seat that smelled like honeysuckle.

"I said I was sorry."

She pulled a dust rag from behind the point of sales counter. "I'm not angry at you." She gently held the cloth to his face just as a voice echoed from a back room Liam hadn't even noticed was there.

"Cyan? Is that you?"

"Damn it," Cyan hissed.

A woman stepped out from behind a dark blue curtain. She had blonde hair like Cyan and similar eyes. She was older, though, frail-looking in her thinness, with sharp-edged cheekbones. Behind her came a woman with frizzy, red hair and freckles, wrapped in sheets of colorful fabric. She nibbled her fingers.

The two women stared at Liam until he said, "Hi."

The blonde grew a wrinkle between her brows. "What did you do to him?"

"Nothing," Cyan said. "We ran into each other, and I may have overreacted."

He took the blood-soaked cloth from Cyan. "It was kind of cool, actually, like a superhero."

The women from the back room stepped forward and circled his chair.

"Liam, this is my mother, Rue, and my Aunt Sybil. This is Liam."

"Nice to meet you both." He pulled the cloth away from his face. "I don't think it's broken."

Cyan crossed her arms in response but looked as though she stood on the tips of her toes. She might have taken off running at any sudden movement.

"Where are you from, Liam?" Rue asked, still circling.

"I grew up in Ireland. Moved to California when I was eighteen. I thought the accent was kind of gone, but Cyan says it's not."

Sybil stood next to his chair and actually looked friendly. "Don't your parents miss you, dear, so far away?"

"They're no longer with us."

"I'm sorry," Cyan whispered.

He looked up at her, in her usual leather jacket and boots, white-blonde braids a bit more of a mess than usual due to her ninja moves outside. "It's all right. They've been gone a long time."

"I suppose you were raised by wolves then?"

"Mother." Cyan scowled.

"No, boarding school… which, depending on the teacher, was comparable."

Sybil giggled, and Rue seemed to soften a bit. Well, she stopped circling his chair at least.

He felt a warm hand on his shoulder and turned to see Sybil above him. "There's a washroom through that curtain. Why don't you go rinse the blood off your face so we can see you properly?"

An odd way to put it, but he smiled nonetheless and did as she said. There were more books behind the curtain, older ones, and a cluttered desk. He ducked beneath amulets and wind chimes that hung from the ceiling. In the tiny bathroom, he finally got a look at himself. Not only did he still have a big Band-Aid on his head from the car crash, but his lips and chin were now covered in red. He looked like a wild beast.

Quickly, he rinsed his face and spit a bit of blood into the sink. He hadn't noticed the dark circles under his eyes until that moment.

When he returned to the front of the bookshop, conversation stopped, which made him assume they'd been talking about him. He glanced around. "This is going to sound odd, I assume, but are you witches?"

The three women froze.

"Who said anything about witches?" Rue asked. Her voice was even, calm, cold.

"It's kind of a joke at the Bistro, I guess, but since there's no such thing as witches…" He shrugged and would have gotten the hell out of there before he said anything else completely inappropriate.

But then, his head.

He gasped as bolts of lightning invaded his brain. Luckily the chair was nearby, because his knees crumpled, but he stayed on his feet with the help of some antique furniture.

Vaguely, he heard the sound of his name from Cyan's lips. Then, her hands were on his face, his forehead, fingers curling against his scalp.

"Liam," she said, closer this time.

The pain dwindled, faster than it ever had before. Even with his eyes closed, he felt her right in front of him, and he leaned his forehead against hers, taking deep breaths. Her small hands cupped his jaw, and she breathed with him… in, out, in, out.

"What the hell was that?" she said.

He stood up straight, and her hands fell away. "Headaches. I get headaches."

"Since the accident?" Rue asked.

"No, longer. Since we moved here. I think it's just allergies."

"Didn't look like allergies," Rue said.

"Well, I feel better now. Maybe you *are* a witch." He smiled and looked down at Cyan, whose skin was the color of the paper she'd dropped earlier.

Rue suddenly pushed him toward the door. "Liam, it was very nice to meet you, but we really need to get the shop open for business."

"Sure. I need to get back to the hospital." He paused before he could be shoved into the street. "Cyan, I got a phone today, so if you don't recognize the number, it's probably just me, waiting to have my ass kicked at Connect Four."

She nodded and looked away before Rue pushed him onto Broad Street, into the morning sun, and slammed the door at his back.

Cyan slumped onto the crooked wooden floor of Sea Books. Sybil knelt and put her hands on Cyan's shoulders, and Rue leaned down to grab her face none too gently.

"You healed him," her mother all but shouted.

Cyan tried breathing, but it didn't work.

Sybil pet her hair and made soothing "shh" noises.

"Hypatia!" Rue yelled.

"Mother," she panted, "you're not… helping."

"Okay." Rue pulled her hands back but stayed close.

Cyan tried again to breathe and was at least able to suck a mouthful or two of air into her lungs before the room started spinning. Rue was right, Cyan had stopped Liam's headache. She'd felt the power go out of her like an invisible vampire sucking life from her veins. She'd felt her palms warm against his scalp. She slumped against Sybil.

"Did you heal him?" Rue asked, arms crossed, thin face pinched in frustration.

"Yes."

Rue put her hand to her mouth and tried to look serious but soon smiled, then chuckled. Cyan looked up at her mother and did the same.

"I have powers," Cyan whispered.

"You have powers," her mother confirmed.

Sybil continued petting her hair. "Then, the Dorcha arrives and War is close."

Both Rue and Cyan stopped smiling.

Sybil leaned forward and kissed Cyan's forehead before disappearing silently to the back room, behind the dark blue curtain.

"I need to call your father," Rue said. She took her phone out the front door of Sea Books and onto the still recovering sidewalks of Charleston's beautiful Broad Street.

That left Cyan alone, legs folded beneath her, on the floor. She lifted her hands and stared at her palms. They appeared the same as they had twenty minutes earlier, and yet, they weren't. They had just healed a man, which meant her powers were manifesting—which meant Sybil was right. No matter the moment of celebration, the Dorcha was somewhere near, which meant Cyan would soon have to fight and possibly die. She was, after all, the Loach of prophecy, and it was her destiny to stop a big, bad dark witch from covering Earth in shadow. Days earlier, she wouldn't have minded dying in battle, but now, after finding Liam?

She covered her face with her hands and was surprised when her palms warmed yet again, the increase in temperature bringing with it a memory of him, his forehead pressed to hers, mouth so close she could have kissed it. And she wanted to—Cyan wanted to kiss Liam. She closed her eyes and focused on the picture painted by her palms: his green eyes staring down at her, his lips parted, and the scent of him, a bit of sweat but mostly remnants of a crisp, clean deodorant or maybe cologne. She wanted to reach beneath his clothes and touch his skin. She wanted his skin on hers, which made her blink and remove her hands from her face.

Rue stepped back in from the street and paused in the doorway, looking down at Cyan as if she had spiders on her face. "You were thinking about him."

"Jesus, Mother." Cyan stood. "Can you not see everything all the time?"

"I didn't need magic to see you were thinking about him," Rue snapped. She cleared her throat. "He's a very attractive young man."

"Don't." She needed some of Sybil's tea, preferably her Cruinn blend, which promised clarity and focus. She needed to think about the scattered papers nearby and not about Liam's mouth, which was lovely, in fact, and looked soft and full and... She shouted Sybil's name.

Her aunt yelped in response but agreed to make the tea.

"What did Daddy say?"

Rue sighed. "That you have a job to do today and that we will work on the Craft tomorrow."

"Good." She went for the hospital records, turned her back on her mother, and joined Sybil in the silence of the back room.

Cyan spent the afternoon going through ancient Craft family trees. She compared the names she found in Sybil's dusty books to the names of victims from the trolley—and survivors, of which there were a few. She found no correlations, but as Rue so helpfully pointed out around noon, a light witch in hiding would probably alter his or her name, especially if they suspected a dark witch was on the hunt.

The Burroughs and Plainacher families had never changed their names to avoid detection, probably because only other witches would ever know what the names meant. Cyan would have liked to have a different last name, only because both Burroughs and Plainacher carried connotations of death. On her father's side was George Burroughs, the only minister executed during the Salem Witch Trials in 1692. As family history explained, George was only suspected due to his immense strength. Of course, he was, in fact, a witch—that much was true—but he was a light witch who mixed his belief in God with his belief in the Craft. He had been harmless, but his strength lived on in the Burroughs men, Drake included.

The Plainacher side, Rue and Sybil's side, had a more sordid history. They were descendants of Elisabeth Plainacher, an alleged Austrian witch and the only person executed for witchcraft in Vienna during the panic of 1583, perhaps with reason. Elisabeth was no minister. In fact, she was a seductress who not only had Sybil's power of second sight but Rue's talent for potions—which, rumor had it—she used to murder the wife of the man she loved. Instead of hiding this surname, though, her family held tight to their heritage for generations.

In truth, Cyan was relieved she at least carried the name of Burroughs as opposed to Plainacher. At least she felt somewhat allied to the good side.

Cyan cussed and jumped in her seat when Rue's hand touched her shoulder. "Careful, Mother, or I'll accidentally bust your nose, too."

"I'm sure you shocked Liam very much with your fighting abilities this morning. You always have been more like your father than me."

Cyan sighed at the level of sadness she heard in that statement.

"Have you found anything?"

"No." Cyan shook her head.

"Maybe you should come join your father and me for dinner at the homestead."

"Not tonight." She ran her hand down the list of deceased tourists. "I must be missing something."

Rue was silent for a moment. "I like him."

"Hmm?"

"Your Liam."

"You didn't act like it."

"I just don't want you distracted, especially if War has arrived."

Cyan curled her blonde braids onto the top of her head and shoved a pencil through her tangled locks until her semi-dreads sat in a tower above her forehead. "The Dorcha is somewhere in Charleston, Mother. I'm focused, all right?" She tapped her fingers on the desk. "Plus, the man is in love with Zoe. Very much in love. I'm not going to fuck with that."

"Language."

Cyan rolled her eyes.

"I'm going home. Don't stay here all night. You need sleep, especially since we're going to test your abilities tomorrow," Rue said.

"Hooray, I can heal headaches."

"You'll soon be doing a lot more than that, and you'll need to know how to control it."

"Goodnight, Mother."

An hour later, Sybil announced she was heading upstairs. She said she needed time to process Cyan's newly arrived abilities as well as Liam's surprise appearance. She said she thought she might paint and left Cyan alone in the dimness of the Sea Books backroom, where not even the orange sunset permeated.

Cyan considered taking a break from the seemingly pointless research into the unfortunate trolley occupants and maybe picking up a book about the healing arts—of which she was an apparent recipient—when her cell phone rang. She didn't recognize the number.

"Hello?" she said.

"I'm sorry I was an idiot today."

"You weren't an idiot."

"I accused your family of being a bunch of witches."

She chortled. "Well, you'd just had your face smashed by a woman half your size. How's your nose?"

"It's fine. Speaking of, are you an actual ninja?"

"No, but my father always insisted I know how to protect myself."

"Well, feel free to inform him that I give you a rave review." He took a deep breath, followed by silence.

"Any… any news on Zoe?" She rubbed her eyes.

"No. The doctors keep telling me it hasn't been long, it hasn't been long, but it feels like she's been in this hospital bed forever."

"Can you sing?"

He chuckled. "No. Absolutely not."

"You should sing to her."

"I don't want to make her feel worse."

"It's that bad?" She leaned back in her chair and rested her big boots on the desk edge.

"In boarding school, our choir director once told me to just mouth the words."

Cyan winced. "Ouch."

"Yeah. He was right, of course. I sound like a screaming donkey."

"I've never heard a screaming donkey."

"I'll sing for you sometime."

She laughed.

"So what did you do today, after kicking my ass?"

She looked at the papers around her. "Just worked at the shop."

"I didn't really get a chance to look around. I'll have to come back someday."

"It's mostly just books about how to look younger and find inner peace. That kind of shit. Some might call it New Age. My mother sells her tinctures—*magic potions*—since we're witches and all."

"You're not going to let me live that down."

"No, you're right, people do say we're witches. My aunt actually does fortune telling sometimes. Three hundred years ago, she probably would have been burned at the stake by now, if only for her bad fashion sense."

"Not everyone call pull off biker babe, Cyan, at least not like you."

"I've never been on a motorcycle in my life."

"Okay, well, not everyone can pull off leather like you."

She chewed her thumbnail and enjoyed the silence.

"Is it strange that I feel like I've known you for years?"

"No," she said.

"The irony is, when Zoe wakes up, you probably won't get along at all. You're nothing like each other."

Cyan didn't say anything.

"Oh, God, I didn't mean that to sound horrible. I just meant you're very different women."

"I'm sure." She thought about the *Book of Shadows,* the prophecy. "No one's like me."

"I think that's true," he said.

"I gotta go, Liam."

"Of course. Hot dinner date?"

His words stung, but she did her best to sound amused. "Wouldn't you like to know?"

She felt his smile through the phone. "Have a good night, Cyan."

"Get some sleep."

"Okay."

After she hung up, she saved his number in her phone. She didn't name him Dof. She named him Liam, because now that her invisible man had a name, she would never forget it.

Chapter Seven

In his dream, he was underwater. Alarms sounded above him, reminiscent of a submarine screaming about incoming missiles. Liam struggled to the surface, holding his breath, until he broke through and found himself not floating in the ocean amidst the wreckage of an exploded warship but instead in a brightly lit hospital room. The alarms didn't stop, and soon, men and women in scrubs descended like a swarm of bees over the unconscious woman in the hospital bed.

"Zoe," he muttered, still half asleep. He shoved himself up from the uncomfortable cot, which was when a nurse finally noticed him. She took hold of his upper arms and pushed him backwards.

"Sir, you need to give the doctors some space."

"Zoe!" he shouted.

The machines around her screamed. The friendly doctor, the one who tried so hard to be helpful, knelt across Zoe's torso and compressed her chest.

"She's flat-lining," someone said.

Liam tried to step forward, but again, the nurse held him tightly and kept him at a distance as he watched the woman he loved struggle to live.

"Come on." He heard the doctor as she continued compressions.

The machine that measured Zoe's heart rate shrieked one high-pitched note.

"No," Liam whispered. "Zoe..."

The doctor mimicked his repetition of Zoe's name, as if she might hear them calling and come back. And then, she did. The heart rate machine blipped once, twice. It kept going, and the doctor hovering over Zoe's chest leaned back, out of breath.

Liam shoved the nurse away and stepped up to the side of Zoe's bed. He took her cold hand in his and kissed it. He told the doctor thank you, but he didn't look at her because he feared he might see pity on her face—or, worse, a lack of hope. She did talk to him a little, said things like *internal bleeding, brain damage, be prepared.*

Once everyone left the room, left him alone, he sat in the chair by Zoe's bed and watched her breathe. He refused to sleep. He tried to build more letters with Connect Four, but his fingers shook so much, he dropped half the game pieces, and they rolled away under Zoe's bed.

He didn't know what time it was, and he didn't care. He pulled out his new phone, and when she answered, she sounded alert.

"Did I wake you?" he said.

"No. What's wrong?"

"She flat-lined, and they brought her back."

"I'll be there in ten minutes." Cyan hung up.

She was true to her word. He heard her combat boots running down the hallway, and then, there she stood, in the hospital room doorway, fully dressed. Her blonde hair was in a huge, curled bun on top of her head, some pieces having fallen free in her mad dash. She was out of breath, and her gray eyes were bright. No, she hadn't been sleeping. He wondered how much Cyan ever slept at all.

"Is she okay?"

Liam didn't rise from the hospital chair. "For now."

Still in the doorway: "What did the doctor say?"

"Be prepared," he whispered.

Cyan's shoes squeaked as she crossed the floor and knelt beside his chair. She didn't touch him. "Doctors don't know shit."

He took her hand and noticed she flinched. "I'm sorry I keep doing this to you, bringing you into this mess. I don't have anyone else."

Slowly, she put her other hand on top of his. "I don't have anyone else either. Not really."

"That can't be true."

"Maybe I've been waiting for you," she said.

Liam looked down at her, taken aback by her words.

Cyan pulled her hand away and sat Indian style next to his chair. Her eyes stared under the bed.

He reached into the front pocket of his jeans and pulled out the item he'd been carrying for over a week. He handed the engagement ring to Cyan, whose hand trembled before curling into a fist around the large, blue diamond and silver band.

"I was going to ask her after the gala. I don't know why I waited. I wasn't nervous." He shook his head. "Maybe if I'd asked her beforehand, we never would have been there. We never would have been on Broad Street."

"How did you meet?"

"I was sommelier at a French restaurant in San Francisco."

"I don't know what that word means."

"Restaurant?"

She smiled. A little.

"Sommelier. It's a fancy word for a wine snob. It wasn't love at first sight. Nothing silly like that. Zoe was a customer, and she liked wine. French rosé at first, until I made her try Bordeaux. She said it tasted like dirt. I said it was just the French funk, part of what makes French wine so good, and she told me I should redefine the word 'good.'" He chuckled, but the amusement felt hollow in his chest. "She asked if she could buy me dinner, which seemed out of character. I thought she was sort of old-fashioned, very proper—a fancy English teacher. I about had a heart attack when she refused to let me pay."

Cyan smiled.

"Before her, I was no good at relationships. I was always so panicky, clingy even. I pushed so many women away, good women, because I was afraid of being alone. I went from relationship to relationship until I met Zoe."

"She was different."

He nodded. "She's stronger than me, more self-assured, even though she lost her parents, too."

"I'm sorry."

"She wasn't. She acknowledged from the start: shit happens. I liked that about her right away. And she didn't make me feel crazy or afraid. I never doubted her for a second. Even when she got the job out here, I never thought she'd leave me. I knew I'd go with her. But I didn't think she'd end up in a hospital bed. She never even gets sick, you know?"

Cyan handed the ring back to him.

"Is there a guy in your life? There's got to be."

"No. I've never had a boyfriend." She wrapped her arms around her knees.

"I know about a dozen guys at the Bistro who'd line up to take you to dinner."

She shook her head. "No, thanks."

"Waiting for Prince Charming?"

Her lip twitched, and she squeezed her eyes shut.

"Did I say something wrong?"

"No."

He slid from his chair and onto the floor. "Then why are you crying?"

She laughed toward the ceiling. "I never cry."

Liam reached out to wipe a tear from the edge of her cheek, and her small hand covered his. She nuzzled against his palm, eyes closed. He froze and let her rub her cheek against his hand. He knew he should feel wrong with Zoe comatose behind him, but something about Cyan made it all so innocent. Perhaps, it was her innocence, because even though she'd smashed his face into pavement the morning before, she seemed untouched and unaware of her own striking sensuality. The thought of this woman being a virgin was shocking, what with the way she looked, talked, walked. She was undeniably sexy, no shrinking violet. Something about her felt powerful.

Just as the thought passed, her skin burned blue. Cyan's eyes popped open as Liam twitched his hand backwards, fell on his ass, and smacked the back of his head against Zoe's hospital bed.

"Shit," he said, hand to his skull. "Did you see that?"

She was on her feet and running before he could even stand. He yelled after her, but the sound of her retreating feet indicated she had no intention of turning back—and he wasn't sure he wanted to follow.

Chapter Eight

It was almost four AM when Cyan reached her parents' ivy-covered house, the house of her upbringing, and she banged on the front door until an alert Drake Burroughs answered, dark brown hair askew. He towered above her. "What is it, little one?"

"Liam," she stuttered. "I need… shit, Daddy." She wrapped her arms around her huge father.

Drake led her inside a clean but disorganized home filled with charms, knickknacks, and decorative pillows. It looked like a beach house, what with all the pastel fabrics and lightwood—and books, everywhere books.

Rue wandered down the staircase barefoot. "What's happening now?"

"I'm not really sure, darling." Drake tried leading Cyan to a chair, but she refused.

Cyan walked away and stood by the bay window that overlooked the family garden. "I need you to heal her."

"Who?" Drake asked.

"Zoe, Liam's… she should be his fiancée, but he didn't get to ask her before the accident. I need you to heal her, Daddy."

"Slow down, child," Drake said in his robe. He sat on the couch. "What on Earth just happened to you?"

"Liam called. Zoe almost died tonight. The doctors are telling him to 'be prepared.'" She scoffed. "As if anyone can be prepared for something like this, even a guy who lost both his parents. You should have seen him. He looked different tonight, like he's dying with her. You need to… please, Daddy, you need to wake her up."

Drake glanced at his wife, who remained standing near the base of the steps with her arms wrapped around her thin shoulders. Rue was powerful, of course. She was good at potions, but Cyan knew her father was the one for this assignment. Drake had his hand in the darker arts and was even known for his curses. Somehow, Cyan felt like her daddy was the one who would need to bring Zoe back—as if he might need to reach into some darkness to find her.

"Do you care about this boy?" Drake asked.

"Yes."

"Do you love him?"

Cyan looked at her mother. "It doesn't matter. Whatever there is between Liam and me—whatever *destiny*—none of that matters. I think if she dies, he'll die with her."

Drake shook his head. "My poor baby girl."

"We don't have time for emotion right now. Right now, I need you to get dressed and do this. Please, Daddy."

After thirty seconds of silence, Drake nodded his head and stood. He disappeared upstairs, kissing his wife on the forehead as he went. Then, Cyan allowed herself to be hugged by her mother—something Rue rarely did.

Father and daughter walked quickly to the hospital but paused near the entrance. He took her wrist in his hand. "You might need to help me," he said. "I know you've been manifesting."

"No, I can't." She pulled her hand away. "I have no control over it. Shit, Liam touched my face earlier, and I glowed blue."

"He saw that?"

"I don't know what he saw, not really. I fucking sprinted out of there."

"Your training starts today. You've got to learn to control yourself, harness whatever powers are awakening in you. I can't have lightning bolts shooting out your fingers in the middle of East Bay Street."

"Fine, yes, but after we do this." She pointed at the hospital.

"I'm gonna cloak us both to be invisible, you hear me? We don't need anyone asking questions. When we get to the room, I'm putting Liam to sleep." He popped the collar on his khaki Carhartt jacket and walked in his heavy work boots toward the entrance. Unlike Cyan's mother, Drake had no need for incantations. He waved his hand and made it so. Sometimes, Cyan wondered just how powerful her soft-spoken father really was. Rue had told her once that he had a kind of sordid past with the Craft. Drake had backed up the claim by saying, simply, "Thank goodness for your mother."

Cyan kissed her grandmother's agate necklace and stepped over the threshold of Charleston Memorial Hospital. No one noticed as they walked by the front desk. No one noticed them on the steps or even lingering outside Zoe's room. Liam, as could be expected, was completely awake and standing near the window. He didn't notice them enter, of course, thanks to Drake's invisibility spell. Cyan watched her father approach Liam, put his hand in front of the young man's face, and, thankfully, catch Liam in his arms. Strong as her daddy was, even Liam looked like a lanky ragdoll in Drake's grip. He laid Liam on the cot by Zoe's bed and turned to the unconscious woman.

Cyan stood at her father's side after casting a single concerned glance at the man she was supposed to love—who was supposed to love her back, according to Sybil. "What now?"

"Hush." Drake pulled out a pocketknife and dug into his palm.

Cyan closed her eyes. "Shit, Daddy." She knew her father used blood in almost all his rituals—the dark side of him showing—but she still never got used to it.

He folded his hand into a fist and opened it again, a thin layer of wet red coating his fingers. A slight bit of gray light burned through the blood and cast Zoe's pale face in moving shadow. He then put his meaty mitt above the center of Zoe's chest, moving up and down in shallow waves. He moved his hand above her face, down to her stomach. Cyan looked up at her father's face, wrinkled in concern. Finally, he said, "Something ain't right."

"What do you mean?"

He moved his hand over Zoe's chest again. "She's not here."

Cyan grabbed her father's arm. "What do you mean, she's brain dead?"

Drake's right eye twitched. "No."

"Then, what the hell do you mean?"

"It's like her soul isn't here." With his uninjured hand, Drake picked up one of Zoe's limp hands and cradled it between his own.

"You're not making any sense."

"Neither is this." His wide brow crinkled.

"Just bring her back."

"I can't bring her back when there's nothing here."

Cyan felt her stomach boiling with annoyance. She pointed at the beeping machines. "Something is here. Someone is here. Look at the damn machines, Daddy. The woman is alive. Her heart is beating."

Drake dropped Zoe's hand. "She feels lost, little girl."

"No," Cyan said. She shook her head. "No. That can't be true." She spun around and knelt next to Liam's cot. She touched his face and ran her hands through his hair. "No," she whispered, watching him sleep. "Please, Daddy. He'll break into a million pieces."

Liam whimpered what sounded like Zoe's name.

Cyan growled and stood. "Dark magic, then. We'll bring her back that way."

Her father's dark blue eyes turned murderous. "I don't touch that anymore, Hypatia, and you damn well know it."

Drake never used that name for his daughter. Never.

She curled her hands into fists and cursed her burgeoning powers—her weak, useless powers. She would soon fight a War against the dark Dorcha, and she wasn't ready. She wanted to help Liam, and she couldn't. She would have called upon the dark spirits to bring Zoe back, but she didn't know how.

She hardly realized she was panting, breaths coming harshly in and out her throat. A heat grew in the center of her chest until she screamed, and the window behind Drake exploded outward into Charleston daybreak.

The next thing she remembered was being carried by someone strong. She recognized the arms beneath her, huge hands cradling her. He'd carried her dozens of times before as a small child, up to bed. Now, he carried her beneath palm trees, beside old buildings. The sky above was the color of violet petals, so the sun would soon rise.

"Daddy," she whined.

"Shh, it's all right."

They arrived outside the entrance of Sea Books, and Drake shouted and banged at the door until Sybil answered in her bedclothes—although by the look of her puffy, red eyes, she hadn't done much sleeping.

She put her hand on Cyan's forehead. "Why is she playing possum?"

"I'm not." Cyan tried shoving away from Drake, who held her even tighter as he stepped into the shop.

"Girl just made a window explode." He set her down in Cyan's favorite dusty chair. "Sybil, I want you to do a reading. Tell me what you see in her right now."

Sybil pulled her red and purple paisley nightgown tight. "Not right now, Drake." Her chocolate eyes moved to the floor.

"Yes, right now," he said. "We need you right now."

Sybil shook her head.

Cyan, still feeling weak, had enough strength to sit up and look at her beloved auntie. "What's the matter, Sybil?"

She smiled softly, sadly. "I had a bit of a bad night, dear."

Cyan found the strength to stand. "Why?"

Sybil tilted her head, still smiling, but her eyes were wet. "The new painting of Liam's in the back."

Cyan shoved her immense father out of the way—some feat—as she passed through the midnight blue curtain and into the secret room of Sea Books and also Sybil's studio. She smelled oils, pungent and familiar. A new painting stood on Sybil's easel, and Cyan rushed toward it only to stop when she saw it.

"No," she whimpered.

The subject of the painting was Liam, of course, as usual, but unlike all the other paintings Sybil had created over the past twenty years—of him smiling, laughing, lit by sun—this was a painting of pain. The dark edges cast his chiseled face in shadow and, though his head tilted downward, it was impossible to miss the pain in his eyes and the tears on his cheeks. His lips were parted in what looked like a silent sob.

"Sybil!" she shouted.

But instead of her aunt responding, she heard an altogether unexpected voice from the front of Sea Books, calling her name. She rushed back out to the front, where she found her father staring at the door and Sybil cowering behind the sales counter as if she could actually feel Liam's pain—because he was in pain. That much was obvious as he stood in the doorway of Sea Books, now drenched in the orange of sunrise. There were no tears in his green eyes, but the emptiness she saw there was worse. His broad shoulders sagged. His lips parted before he spoke as though his mouth was ready but the words were not.

"My Zoe's gone," he said.

Cyan shook her head.

"I heard glass break. I woke up, and the room was in chaos—the broken window, the alarms and beeping machines. It was too late." His empty eyes looked at Sybil. "It was like her spirit flew out into the morning light."

Sybil made a choking sound of despair and Cyan wondered how much Sybil, as a seer, could feel of Liam's pain.

He stepped quickly toward Cyan and grabbed her upper arms. "Are you a witch?" He shook her, just a little. "I saw blue light coming off of you. If you're really a witch, you have to bring her back. Right now. You have to." He shook some more until Drake put his hand on Liam's shoulder.

"I can't," Cyan said. "My daddy tried."

Liam let go of her and shrugged Drake's hand from his shoulder. He crumpled into the nearest chair and stared at the floor. "So you are witches, then?"

Cyan glanced at Drake, who gave the slightest nod. "Yes," she said.

Liam coughed on a horribly twisted chuckle. "Can you do anything about my pain?"

He didn't speak of anything physical—Cyan knew that much—and her father could easily work a spell like that, something to emotionally numb Liam, just for a little while, but something warm stirred within Cyan. She held her hand out in front of her father and approached Liam where he sat.

She straddled his lap, shoving his back against the chair. He looked up at her, eyes no longer empty. Pain rushed in along the edges.

Cyan focused. She put both her hands on his jaw and tilted his face toward hers. She felt something powerful burning in her chest and did what instinct dictated: she kissed Liam on the mouth. She even opened his mouth with her tongue—something she didn't even know how to do under normal circumstances.

He didn't struggle beneath her, but he didn't move to reciprocate the kiss either.

When she swallowed a breath of him, she tasted his broken heart. She sucked on his mouth, pulling, pulling, until her chest ached with the cold. Tears ran down her face, but she kept kissing Liam, kept sucking the pain from his body, until she tumbled from his lap and onto the floor.

Cyan heard a mixture of voices saying her name, but it was Liam's touch she recognized first, checking her pulse. Sobbing, she opened her eyes and stared at him, wondering how one person could hold so much pain without being poisoned by it, without dying.

Her father brought a blanket and tossed it over Cyan as Liam lifted her into his arms and cradled her small, shaking form against his chest. "Thank you," he said. "Thank you, my little witch."

Chapter Nine

With Drake Burroughs at his side, Liam watched Cyan sleep fitfully on a threadbare couch in the back of Sea Books. She mumbled to herself and pulled the blanket closer. The aunt, Sybil, had been sent away to find Rue, Cyan's mother, plus a cornucopia of healing herbs from the family homestead garden.

Despite his physical injuries sustained in the car crash and the huge emotional hole left by Zoe's sudden death, Liam felt nothing—just a vague sense that he should. Somehow, the little blonde witch with the long braids had sucked all feeling out of him. He still tasted her on his mouth like sweet tea.

Liam jumped at the sound of Drake's voice. "That spell she cast won't last long."

"Is she okay?" The way Cyan's eyes twitched reminded him of a small animal having a nightmare.

"She will be," her father said, "although that was some powerful juju she just pulled on you, boy. Even I can't do that trick. Could have killed her."

"I thought only women were witches."

"No. The most powerful ones usually are, though." Drake paused. "Women are stronger than us, so more powerful, too."

"Cyan said she tried to heal Zoe."

"No, that would have been me."

Liam turned and stared into the dark blue eyes of Drake Burroughs, a man who looked like he could tear a phone book in half, maybe two. "So why didn't you?"

Drake stood even taller. "I tried, but by the time Cyan took me to your Zoe, she was already gone. Her soul was, at least. That broken window that woke you was thanks to my little girl's temper." He nodded at Cyan, who whimpered.

Liam tried to stand as tall as Drake, but that was impossible—Drake was too damn big. He tried to at least hold his shoulders back and his head high. "Bring Zoe back from the dead."

"We don't do dark magic around here. We're light witches, not necromancers."

"I don't give a shit what you are. Bring her back."

Drake took hold of the front of Liam's shirt and shoved him backwards until he hit the wall. The nearby bookshelf shuddered, and dust tumbled down around them. "You know why you're here? You know why your woman is dead? Because of dark magic. Because some crazy dark witch flipped that trolley on Broad Street. You want to put your trust in someone like that? For all you know, that dark witch would just put a different soul in Zoe's body—a dark soul—and watch it run amok. You like that idea? Your Zoe coming back as a murderer?"

Liam shoved Drake away, although his shove only moved the man back about six inches. He let go of Liam's shirt at least. "A dark witch caused the accident?"

Drake inclined his head. "Cyan saw it."

"I did, too." Liam shuffled away and sat in the nearest armchair.

"Huh?"

"A red flash. I thought it was an explosion. Did you find the witch who did it?"

"We're looking for him."

"Then, what will you do? When you find him?"

Drake shook his head. "Well, we're not calling your ass, if that's what you're asking. We're not in the business of revenge, boy. You got no business in our world anyway."

"How many witches are there?"

"Plenty," Drake said. "But that girl right there." He nodded to Cyan. "She's something special."

"I feel like I've known your daughter my whole life. Is that strange?"

Drake's right eye twitched.

"Is there something you're not telling me?"

"There's a whole lot of things I'm not telling you." His voice softened. "Look. Liam. You have business to take care of at the hospital. You got grieving to do. Now, like I said, this spell you're under right now, the numbness, it ain't gonna last long, so you take care of your business before you remember the pain. Then, you go home and start drinking. I mean, drinking hard, until you forget about all this." Drake gestured to Cyan, the back room of Sea Books, and the cloud of dust that still danced in gold lamplight. "Don't come looking for us until we come looking for you."

"Why would you come looking for me?" Liam asked.

Drake shook his head and turned his back. "You can't tell anyone about what you've seen here today. You can't tell anyone about us, or the repercussions will be dire."

Liam heard the threat, but it didn't affect him in the least. "Who would believe me?"

"In this town? Plenty of folk. Plenty of folk already suspect, some know, and others are witches themselves."

"Shit," he muttered.

"Welcome to Charleston, Liam Cody. Now, you better hightail it before the women get back and start tutting all over you."

He stood and extended his hand toward Cyan. "Is she going to be okay?"

"Yeah. As the spell wears thin, your pain will leave her and come find you, so like I said, start drinking. I think you deserve that much. I know if I lost my Rue…" Drake looked toward the floor. "Well."

"Tell her thank you," Liam said.

Drake nodded but didn't speak and also didn't offer Liam an escort to the exit.

He did go back to the hospital. He dealt with so-called "business," all the while surrounded by nurses and the kind doctor who'd been there for him from the start. There was paperwork and legalities and vague discussions of a will—although, he was told, all that would be taken care of in time. For the moment, Liam was told to surround himself with friends, of which he had none, except perhaps Cyan, but he'd just been basically banished from her doorstep.

He walked out of the hospital into a cool November morning in Charleston, the city he once found to be beautiful but no longer. The waving palm trees seemed to dance to a funeral dirge. The sunlight and blue sky taunted him.

"It should be dark," he whispered.

He walked back downtown and found the only liquor store open at 10 AM. He bought a bottle of scotch—the same stuff his boss Max had brought him at the hospital. Then, Liam began the slow walk to the expensive condo that would never be home again, not without Zoe. When he entered, the house smelled like her perfume, and he heard the ghost of her laugh as he fell into the couch, bottle already open in his hand. He took three long drags until he coughed. He still felt numb, although around the edges of his mind, the pain had begun to creep like claws in his skull. He drank more scotch.

He drank until he started to forget things, wiping his mind clean as he eventually felt the slow pull of blackout and finally sleep.

He dreamt of Zoe. He saw the empty bottle of scotch on the refurbished coffee table they'd picked up at an antique store near the Charleston Market. The bright sunlight through windows foretold early afternoon. He wore the same dark jeans and wrinkled shirt from the morning when the hospital machines screamed and, then, went dead. Yet, Zoe stood in front of him in a white nightgown, her long, brown hair in waves around her naturally milk-white complexion.

"Zoe?" he croaked.

She lifted her long nightgown up above her knees and slid onto his lap with her hands on his shoulders.

"You're dead."

Her hands felt warm against his face as she tilted his head back and kissed him hard. Her fingers ran through his hair and settled on the back of his neck, pulling him closer. She moaned and unbuttoned his shirt, shoving the fabric away to better reach his chest. One thing Zoe had never hidden: she adored Liam's body—the lean musculature and sparse, brown hair. She even once said she was jealous of his long legs.

Liam's head felt fuzzy, confused, as his dead girlfriend slid down his body until she knelt between his legs. She pushed his knees apart while kissing his abdomen.

"Zoe, what—"

She glanced up at him before unbuttoning his jeans.

He leaned forward and tangled his fingers in the back of her hair. "You're not here," he said. "You're not." The air shook in his throat as he tried to inhale.

"You're right." She smiled. "I'm dead."

Liam gasped into consciousness, leaping forward on the couch. He heaved for breath but instead of oxygen, filled his mouth with scotch. He enjoyed the painful burn but Cyan's spell had worn off and the pain was back in all its vindictiveness. He drank more and thought he should have bought two bottles, because one wouldn't be enough to fill the hole in his chest. He thought he should be bleeding. He should have a visible wound. How was it possible to be this tormented by invisible pain? How would he walk? How would he talk? How would he live, like this?

Chapter Ten

Cyan's head ached when she moved and she heard her daddy's voice, very close, whispering, "Easy."

Cyan groaned again when she felt a hand on her forehead.

"Don't push our little girl now, darling," Drake's voice sounded from above her.

"Cyan," Rue yelled, despite her husband's entreaty.

She used all her strength to lift her eyelids and look up into the worried faces of her family.

Rue, long blonde hair pulled back, pushed a chalice toward her. "Drink this. Now."

Cyan shifted up on the couch in the back room of Sea Books enough to take the stinky tincture and sip. She made a disgusted face.

"All of it," Rue commanded.

Cyan took the rest of her mother's magic mix back like a shot of cheap tequila.

"Now, sit up."

"Rue." Drake crossed his arms.

Sybil lingered nearby, smelling of honeysuckle.

"That spell you did could have killed you, swallowing that sort of pain," Rue just about shouted.

Cyan pushed herself up to sitting. "Where's Liam?"

Rue's pointed finger almost touched the tip of her nose. "You will not be thinking about that boy right now. We've got much more important things to deal with than your romantic feelings for that Dof."

Cyan winced a little at the old Gaelic nickname for her invisible man—the man her psychic Aunt Sybil had painted since Cyan's childhood, the man she was destined to love and be loved by in return.

"Where is he?" Cyan said.

"I sent him home, little girl," Drake said. "He's got his own problems right now, as do we. Your powers are, well, impressive." Her daddy paused as if considering "impressive" an understatement. "We need to harness them immediately. And the strength at which they're growin' makes me think the Dorcha is very close."

"No shit, Daddy." Begrudgingly, she decided Liam could wait. "What do we do?"

"Tests." Rue stood, her long skirts swinging around her. She took the now empty chalice from Cyan's hand and walked barefoot to a rickety table near the back bookcase. She brushed off a cloud of incense ash and set the glass down before stepping away. "Your father said you shattered an entire damn window at the hospital. Shatter this."

"Rue," Sybil whispered.

"Sybil, I'm her mother. Cyan." She gestured to the glass.

Frankly, Cyan had no idea how to shatter anything. The thing at the hospital had been brought on by rage. Thinking back, every time her magic had manifested so far had involved some emotion. Thinking deeper, every manifestation had involved some emotion related to Liam: the need to heal him, protect him, love him. She knew the Craft required emotion—at least the more powerful spells—but she should be able to break a glass. Shouldn't she?

She stood and focused on the empty chalice. She already felt better physically and emotionally, thanks to whatever potion her mother had forced her to drink. Cyan stared at the glass and told it to break. She recited old spells in her head. She even repeated some magic words out loud, but nothing happened.

Cyan shook her head. "Nothing. Again. As usual."

Rue threw up her hands. Sybil fell onto the couch where Cyan had recently slept. Only Drake Burroughs remained calm. He put his big mitts on his daughter's shoulders. "As a family, we've agreed we can't have Liam around you right now. Your feelings for him will weaken you against the Dorcha, but maybe the thought of him will make you strong."

"What are you talking about, Daddy?"

"Drake," Sybil said softly. "Let me."

Her father moved away, replaced by the red frizzy head of her meek, diminutive aunt. Sybil held one of Cyan's hands and told her to close her eyes.

"See Liam in your mind, sweetheart. See him looking happy."

Cyan tried, but all she could see was his grief. "I can't."

When Sybil let go of her hand, Cyan opened her eyes and watched her aunt's retreating back, heard the sound of her many bracelets. It wasn't long before Sybil returned with a painting. It was not the awful, tragic one she'd painted just the night before—the night Liam lost the love of his life. This was an older painting of Liam in the sun, smiling in the black and white oil of all Sybil's visionary art.

Sybil held the painting in front of her. "See this young man. And focus."

Cyan stared at smiling Liam. Her fingertips touched the painted edge of his mouth. A bit of warmth stirred in her belly, but she wasn't sure if that was magic or the way Liam made her feel just being himself. Slowly, she looked toward the chalice, but instead of shattering, it weakly shook and tumbled to its side.

"Fuck!" Cyan pulled her own hair.

Even Rue didn't yell at her for "language."

"It's like I can't do a damn thing without him right in front of me."

"You can't just handcuff him to you for the duration of the War," Rue spat.

"I'm trying!" Cyan screamed. She looked around the room and wanted to tear it apart—all the books, the charms, the things she'd studied her whole life. None of it meant anything anymore. All that preparation, and for what? The only person who made her magic work was also the only person she wanted to keep safe, away from dark witches and the as yet unidentified Dorcha with his ominous red light.

"Just breathe, little girl," Drake said.

"You're right. I need air." Without saying goodbye, she stomped past her family, out through the front of Sea Books, and onto Broad Street, where rubble from the trolley tragedy no longer desecrated her fine city. In fact, looking down the length of Broad at all the beautiful, old buildings with their wide windows and marble steps, she never would have believed the carnage unless she'd seen it for herself—which she had—the same night she first saw Liam.

She walked, hating everything. She almost ran over tourists on corners, holding maps. Her leather jacket kept her warm against the late autumn breeze, and her anger managed to carry her quickly to the Church of St. Agnes on Meeting Street and Grandmother Plainacher's grave. It was a monstrous piece of marble, completely ostentatious, but Grandmother had been no different. The stone listed her grandmother's name, dates of birth and death, and two simple words: "Blessed be." Cyan curled into fetal position at its base and wrapped her arms around her skinny knees.

"What the hell am I supposed to do now?" she whispered.

The pounding on his front door made Liam's whole brain shake. "Shit." He winced, sitting up and immediately regretting it. An empty bottle of scotch sat on the table in front of him, and based on the light outside, it was early evening. Liam wiped at the side of his mouth, sticky with residual drool, and stood, almost falling over. Was it possible to be hung-over at six PM? He supposed so, but this felt worse than a hangover. He felt sick, maybe even feverish. He put his hand to his forehead and found it sticky with sweat.

The pounding continued.

"Who is it?" Liam shouted.

"It's Max! You weren't answering your phone."

Liam sighed and opened the door.

Max, his boss and manger at Broad Street Bistro, barreled inside. He was dressed for work in a fancy suit. His bald head shined, and he smelled like spicy aftershave. "I'm so sorry, Liam."

"What?" He rubbed his eyes and then remembered—remembered everything. He barely made it to the bathroom before he threw up. He threw up until he choked and then fell onto the floor. Max stood in the doorway. "How did you hear?"

"I went to the hospital. Why didn't you call?"

Liam chuckled. "It didn't seem to matter."

"You shouldn't have been alone."

He thought about the witches at Sea Books.

Max crouched down in front of him. "What do you need?"

His arm still leaning on the toilet, Liam said, "You could get me another bottle of scotch, I guess."

"You only drink scotch when I force it on you."

"Got any with you?" The words flowed together, Liam still drunk from earlier consumption that not even a several hour-long nap could cleanse.

Max pulled a flask from the front of his suit and handed it to Liam, who drank greedily. "You look like hell," Max said.

"I ought to."

"The funeral?"

Liam drank more scotch. "I haven't gotten there yet. Just had to sign some paperwork this morning. Then, Drake told me to drink."

"Who's Drake?"

"Cyan's father. He told me to start drinking. Thought maybe I'd forget some of the…" He held the flask up in toast. "But I remember."

"Liam, you're not making sense."

"Witches."

"Witches?"

Liam took another sip of scotch. "They're not real." He chuckled. "Zoe was real. I was gonna marry her, you know? I have the ring. But you can't marry a dead person."

Max looked like he wanted to reach a hand out, but he didn't. "Liam. Maybe you should go to the hospital."

"I've spent plenty of time at the hospital, thank you. They don't help people there." Max helped Liam stand and put a hand to his forehead.

"You feel like you're on fire."

He pushed Max's hand away. "Yes, maybe I'll chug some NyQuil. There's alcohol in that, too, and Drake said to drink."

Liam stumbled back to the couch and fell face-first, dropping Max's flask along the way. It clunked across the wooden floor. He heard Max pick it up and the quiet slide of metal over expensive fabric.

"Is it possible I was wrong about you?" Max said, standing over him.

"Oh, I dunno," Liam said into the couch cushion. "What did you think about me?"

"That you were stronger than this."

"Go fuck yourself."

Max didn't say anything for a long time, but Liam felt him still standing there.

"What?"

"I'll come back to check on you."

"Don't," Liam mumbled. He closed his eyes to the sound of Max's dress shoes across the floor, followed by the sound of the front door closing. He opened them when the room started to spin. Liam crawled to the bathroom and threw up some more. His final sensation before unconsciousness was the chill of tile against his cheek.

Chapter Eleven

After a cool catnap on her grandmother's tombstone, Cyan rose with the sunset and wandered back to Sea Books, dodging half-drunk locals as she went. The city had officially entered happy hour, but as she turned onto Broad Street, she saw shoppers were still out and about, too.

Sybil almost jumped out of her hand-woven, multi-colored dress when Cyan shoved the front door open.

"You okay?" she asked her aunt.

"Hmm? Yes."

"You sure?"

Sybil rolled a piece of red hair between her fingers and didn't look at her niece. "Fine."

Cyan shimmied out of her leather jacket, only then noticing it was covered in dead leaves. She sighed. "Where's Mother?"

"Hmm?"

"Sybil, what's going on?"

"Nothing?" She dusted the point of sales counter with her own clothing.

"Nothing question mark?" Cyan tossed her jacket onto a chair and shoved through the midnight blue curtain that led to the secret back room.

"Wa-wait!"

Her aunt was too late. Sitting in the center of the desk was the antique Plainacher scrying mirror, a bowl of herbs at its side. Cyan pointed at the black mirror. "Who was my mother looking at?"

"I… it's…" Sybil shook her head and pulled an awkward smile.

Cyan took a deep breath and stared at the mirror. It did nothing but stare back, its surface coal black and unresponsive.

"It's nothing, dear. Why don't you go meet your father for dinner?"

Cyan took a step closer and, having studied Craft texts her whole life, knew the words to make a scrying mirror behave. She began to recite, slowly, although she had no name, because she knew not whom her mother had sought. Behind her, she heard Sybil scramble away.

Cyan didn't really expect anything to happen, because her powers were meek when Liam wasn't there to evoke *feelings*, but she still tried to focus. When she heard Rue's voice in the midst of her own incantations, she froze. Her mother said the same incantations followed by, clearly, the words, "Liam Cody."

"Liam Cody," Cyan said, and wind whipped around her. She closed her eyes against the sudden gale, and when she opened them, she stood in a clean, white kitchen, her mother at the sink with her back turned. "Holy shit!" Cyan hooted.

Her mother spun around and screamed. Then, she put her hand on her chest and sucked breath into her lungs. "Hypatia," she said.

Cyan turned in a circle in the unfamiliar room. "Beam me up, Scotty. Damn!"

Rue's voice was high-pitched and stretched thin. "Where did you come from?"

"The back room of Sea Books. I saw you'd been using the scrying mirror—"

Rue pushed blonde hair off her forehead. "Yes, to find you, but Grandmother's amulet keeps you hidden."

"Duh. But then, I heard your voice. I heard you say Liam's name."

"Yes. I thought you might have gone to him."

"So I said Liam's name, and poof, I just showed up in a kitchen. Where are we?"

Rue leaned back against the kitchen counter, covered in herbs and a small bowl. "You just apparated here?"

"Apparently apparated!"

Rue rolled her eyes and turned back to her herbs.

"Mother. Where is here?"

Rue didn't speak, just kept working, so Cyan looked toward the fridge and saw one photo, hung by a magnet of the Golden Gate Bridge. She recognized Liam immediately, but it took her a moment to understand the beautiful, smiling brunette was his Zoe. Cyan had only seen her after …

"We're at Liam's house?"

Rue stopped moving her mortar and pestle. "Yes."

"Why?"

"When I went looking for you in the scrying mirror—a pointless endeavor—I looked for Liam, as well, and I saw him. Unconscious on his bathroom floor."

Cyan didn't speak, but she moved. She wandered through the unfamiliar condo, darkened by the lack of sun, until she found a brightly lit bathroom covered in white tile and black accents. Liam lay on his side, legs curled up with a blanket over him. His forehead shined with sweat, and he shook.

"Liam?"

"He's not responsive right now," Rue said from the doorway.

Cyan didn't ask about calling for an ambulance. She didn't believe in traditional medicine, not really, but she did believe in whatever liquid cocktail Rue held in her hand. "What did you make him?"

"It's a Glan tincture."

Cyan recognized the Gaelic word for "clean."

"He's been drinking. There's physical and emotional poison running through him, and I plan to clean it out."

"Why do you care about him?"

"Stupid girl." Rue rolled her gray eyes. "Because I care about *you*."

"Well, we can't just leave him on the floor," Cyan said as her mother knelt by her side.

"He was too heavy to move by myself."

"Why didn't you call Daddy?"

Rue put a hand to Liam's face and turned his limp, heavy head toward them. "Because your father is the fool who told this boy to start drinking. He's sleeping at the home of a work friend this evening."

"Mother—"

"You don't say a word to me until you're married, girl. Now, move back."

Cyan slid back on her knees across tile. She watched her mother part Liam's lips and pour the Glan tincture down his throat. He didn't react at all. Rue stood and set the small cup on the counter beside a wine glass that looked like it'd been there for days.

"Now," she said, "we move him. You take his arms."

Liam was really heavy. A series of unladylike grunts and groans got them halfway across the living room before they had to put him down and rest.

Rue huffed. "Feels like the boy has rocks in his tummy."

"Come on," Cyan said. "Let's just get him to the couch." She took tight hold of his wrists but almost dropped him when he moaned softly, and the place where her hand met his skin glowed blue. Cyan looked up at her mother, her thin arms wrapped around Liam's ankles.

"So your magic glows blue then," Rue said.

"Yeah."

"All right. Come on."

They heaved and groaned until finally dropping Liam onto the couch.

"Good golly." Rue sat in the puffy white chair at the end of his sofa. "You'll have to stay with him for a while. Give him another dose of the Glan."

Cyan knelt on the floor and looked at Liam's pale, sweating face. "Mother. Could you use the scrying mirror to see the Dorcha?"

"We need a name to use the scrying mirror. That we do not have. And another thing: you will not apparate again."

"I didn't mean to."

"That worries me even more. You know how dangerous it is."

She put her hand on Liam's. "I got here fine."

"Sure, this time. Next time, you might show up missing an arm."

Cyan ran her thumb over the back of Liam's cold, clammy knuckles. "Momma?"

"You haven't called me that in years."

"The family agreed I shouldn't be around Liam right now. Said he would weaken me against the Dorcha. So why are you asking me to stay with him?"

Rue pursed her lips together in annoyance. "Well, you decided to show up, didn't you?" She sighed. "Anyway, I guess you can sit here with him and practice. If you think this boy holds some key to your power, then…" She waved her delicate hand in the air. "Let him help for now. Be of some use while he's drowning himself in liquor. Damn that Drake Burroughs."

Cyan tried not to smile at the obvious love behind her mother's annoyance.

Rue pushed herself to standing, barefoot, as usual. "There's another dose of Glan on the kitchen counter. Give it to him in four hours. That ought to do the trick."

"Okay."

Her mother lifted her purse from the table by Liam's front door. "And go home in the morning. You smell like a cemetery." She closed the door behind her.

Liam woke on his stomach on the couch wondering why he was on the couch and not in his bedroom. He tried to swallow and found his mouth dry. *Oh,* he realized, *must have been drinking.* He and Zoe rarely overindulged, but it did happen on occasion. He opened his eyes and saw the back of her head in front of him. She was sitting on the floor between their couch and coffee table, brown hair in her eyes, although he could see her soft smile as she read a book.

"Zoe."

She pushed her hair behind her ear and looked at him, brown eyes fond.

"I feel awful." He tried to sit up, but her hands held him down. "Am I sick?"

She tilted her head and kissed him.

"Uh-uh," he said, smiling. "More." He pulled her mouth back to his and kissed, kissed, even when her hands pushed at his chest and tried to shove him away.

"Liam!" she shouted against his mouth.

He held firm.

"Liam, wake up!"

He blinked his eyes and found he held not to his Zoe but to a panicked-looking pale woman with bright blonde braids and light eyes. As soon as he pulled his hands away, she scooted backwards on the floor, her combat boots squeaking across hardwood.

"Cyan?"

She looked away from him, hands curled into fists on the floor.

"Zoe's dead," he said. "Isn't she?"

Cyan's expression softened. "Yes."

Liam tried to sit up but couldn't. Instead, as stomach cramps threatened to make him scream, he curled into a ball. "What's the matter with me?"

"My mother came here and found you like this. She thinks maybe a bit of alcohol poisoning mixed with fever. She gave you a tincture that should help."

"Alcohol poisoning." He winced. "That's funny, because all I can think about right now is chugging a bottle of expensive wine. Could even be cheap wine. I really don't give a shit." His teeth chattered.

Cyan leaned forward cautiously and put her hand on his forehead. "Why aren't you getting better? You should be getting better." She pulled the blanket, already in his lap, up over his shoulders and guided his head back to the pillow.

"Could you get me a glass of water? Please."

She nodded and walked toward his kitchen. He thought it should have felt strange having her there with Zoe on a cold slab in the hospital morgue but he was glad to not be alone in the dark—and he was glad it was Cyan who was with him.

She returned and handed him a cool glass of water, which he consumed quickly. "Are you my watch dog then?"

"I guess." She sat on the floor in front of the couch. "Although I have been practicing."

"Practicing for what?"

Her brow furrowed, and she played with the shoelaces of her boots. "It's kind of a long story."

"Amazingly enough…" He had trouble swallowing. "I have some time."

"You should be sleeping."

"If your story's boring enough, maybe I will."

She shook her head, more at his joke than in refusal. "A witch caused the trolley accident."

"Your father told me."

She glanced at him. "There's this old prophecy in the Celtic *Book of Shadows*. It speaks of the rise of a dark witch and also a light witch, who will save the day. It's the Dorcha versus the Loach in a great War."

"The Dorcha is bad. The Loach is good."

Cyan nodded. "The prophecy is obnoxiously vague, but we do know the lifelines of the Dorcha and Loach will transect."

"How does it go exactly?"

She seemed hesitant to tell him, as though revealing some grand secret, and perhaps she was—some secret of witches.

"You don't have to tell me."

"It's all about murder and death." She wrapped her arms around her knees. "Before I was born, my grandmother foretold that I was the Loach, which meant the Dorcha was alive somewhere, as well. My father suspects the dark witch who flipped the trolley might be the Dorcha, which would explain why my powers have arrived."

"What do you mean, *arrived*?"

"I didn't have any powers until the accident. In fact, the first spell I ever cast was to get rid of your headache."

"I don't understand," he said, although he wondered if that was partially due to the slow rock of the room, back and forth, back and forth.

"Part of the prophecy states the powers of the Loach won't show up until the Dorcha makes an appearance. Their powers feed off each other."

"And what of this War?"

"The Dorcha wants to cover the world in darkness. The Loach has to stop him."

"Kill him."

She nodded.

"Good," Liam said. "He took Zoe."

Cyan stared. He wondered if he'd said something wrong but then realized he didn't care. He'd be willing to kill this Dorcha himself—if he thought he stood half a chance against a man who could flip an entire trolley with the power of magic.

"So witches are different, have different powers?"

"My mother is good with potions. My aunt is a seer. My daddy works some dark magic but nothing bad."

He pulled the blanket tighter around himself, frozen from head to toe. "And you?"

"Well, I've gotten really good at moving that fork over there."

He followed her line of sight and saw one of the forks from his kitchen in the middle of his living room floor. "Show me."

Cyan's gray eyes focused on the fork, and it spun in a rapid circle. "Ta-da," she said without enthusiasm.

"You can do a lot more than that," he said.

"Only when you're—" She stopped talking.

A long period of silence followed. Even the city outside abided.

"What do I have to do with all this, Cyan?"

She stood. "You should sleep."

"What aren't you telling me?"

"I'm not telling you a lot of things."

She sounded just like her father.

"And it's for your own good," she continued. "I'm going to give you your second dose of Glan."

"What the hell is Glan?"

Her nose wrinkled in amusement. "It's a potion. It's supposed to clean you out."

"That sounds messy."

"Not that kind of clean." She spoke from the kitchen, where her voice echoed against marble and tile. "Think of it as detox from all the booze my daddy told you to drink." She came back with a coffee cup. "Drink this. It doesn't taste good."

"Neither does my mouth." He took the potion like a shot and choked on what resembled putrid swamp water. "Ugh. Can I at least brush my teeth?"

"Can you walk?"

"Maybe with some assistance."

She took the cup from him, set it on the nearest table, and then helped him to standing. He weaved a little, but despite her small stature, Cyan kept him steady. She got him all the way to the bathroom, where she gave him privacy to brush his teeth and change his contacts—long overdue, and he was damn near blind without them. He tried to avoid looking at his own reflection in the mirror, but even a cursory glance proved how much he resembled a walking corpse. He looked at the toilet and vaguely remembered throwing up. Max had been there, hadn't he? It all seemed like a faraway blur, as did the wine glass on the counter. He almost crumbled when he saw that.

He always drank wine with Zoe—wine had brought them together, after all—and this was the last evidence of their habit, the last glass she would ever bring him. Reverently, he scooted the glass back against the mirror, unwilling to throw it away.

Cyan returned to his side when he stepped into the living room and guided him onto the couch. He fell heavily, and she tucked the edges of his blanket around his shoulders. "You'll be fine in the morning," she said.

He laughed. "No, I won't."

Chapter Twelve

Liam was right. He wasn't fine in the morning. In fact, he was nonresponsive and didn't wake up even after Cyan smacked him across the cheek. Still shaky on her own Craft technique, she called her mother, who brought Drake along, too. Rue, clad in an artful robe and long dress, hurried into Liam's apartment with a bag of trinkets over her back. She didn't waste even a single glance on her daughter but headed directly for the incredibly ill young man on the sofa.

Cyan watched Rue put her hand on Liam's forehead. "You gave him the Glan tincture, both doses?"

"Yes, Mother."

Drake, dressed for work at the construction site, rubbed his daughter's back—possibly in an effort to ease the way Rue yelled at her.

"Well, then, what in God's name?" Rue sighed and stared at Liam's pale, sweaty face. His breath was shallow and shaky. She put her hand on his head again and closed her eyes.

"Is she reading him?" Cyan whispered.

"Trying to," her daddy said, "by the looks."

She understood her mother was trying to scan Liam's body—not an easy task—and find the cause of his illness. Sometimes, the technique worked, but it was difficult, even for a powerful witch, to touch someone and see exactly what he or she needed.

After about thirty seconds, Rue's hand flew backwards as though burned. Drake let go of his daughter and rushed to his wife. "Rue?"

"Shh." She dug around in her bag. She pulled out a small bottle with a cork in the top and started talking to it—talking to the bottle.

Cyan knew better than to ask.

Rue put her thumb on Liam's chin and pulled until his lips parted. She uncorked her little bottle and held it close to his mouth, and on one of his exhales, a tumultuous black cloud spread like a thunderclap through the room.

Rue fell back onto the ground, almost dropping the bottle. Drake reflexively ducked the dark cloud that quickly dissipated, and Cyan stood there, staring.

"What the hell was that?" she said.

"Christ on a cracker." Rue stared at Liam.

"Daddy?"

Drake looked back at his daughter, brow furrowed so deep, his eyebrows almost blocked his eyes. "He's under a spell, little girl."

"What? Well, I didn't—"

Drake shushed her by holding up his hand. "This ain't a spell you coulda done."

Rue shook her head. "It's a potion. He must have been slipped something." She sighed. "He's not sick, he's going through magic withdrawal."

Cyan stepped closer and stared down at the shivering, unconscious man on the sofa. "Who would slip Liam a potion?"

"That's what we need to find out." Rue stood and brushed her hands off on her dress. "Drake."

True to form, her daddy answered his wife's silent command and slit his palm with his pocketknife. He held his hand above Liam's chest.

"Daddy, what are you—"

A flash of silver-gray light shot from Drake's palm and into the center of Liam's chest. Liam's body jumped, his eyes popped open, and he coughed.

"Shit, Daddy!" Cyan shoved her father out of the way and grabbed for Liam, who continued to choke and moan, bent over on the couch.

"It was just a slight electric shock," Drake said.

Liam pulled gasping breaths of air into his lungs, and Cyan held his head in her hands, her eyes shooting daggers at big Drake Burroughs.

He shrugged. "At least he's awake."

"Fucking hell." Liam put his hand to his forehead and mumbled, "What happened? What's going on?"

"Language," Rue said.

Liam looked up at her. "Huh?"

She shook her head. "Boy, you are not sick. You're under a spell."

"Well—what? From one of you?" He looked to Cyan.

"Not from one of the people in this room, but yes, from one of our kind. Someone has given you a potion, possibly more than once. Has anyone slipped you anything recently?"

He leaned against Cyan and spoke into the fabric of her shirt. "What, like a roofie?"

Rue scoffed, but Cyan saw her daddy smirk.

"Has anyone offered you a drink recently?" Drake asked.

Liam was silent for a moment, shivering with one of Cyan's arms around his shoulders. "Max. I had some of Max's scotch yesterday. Was that yesterday? What day is it? He carries a flask. I had some at the hospital, too. He brought it for me specifically."

Cyan, inexperienced with embracing someone, comforting them, continued to hold her arm stiffly around Liam's upper body. "Who's Max?"

"He's the owner of the Bistro. Max Henny."

"Whoever caused the accident… the red flash of light on Broad Street came from the alley next to the Bistro," Cyan said.

Her parents stood silently, staring at her and then, each other.

"Max?" Liam whispered.

Cyan unconsciously held him closer. "Why would a witch put a spell on Liam?"

"Maybe this Max fellow learned of Liam's connection to you," Drake said.

"What connection? You mean the car accident?"

Cyan opened her eyes wide and gawked at her father as if to say, "Nicely done, you damn fool."

"Drake," Rue barked. "Call Sybil. Tell her to bring the crystal ball. I want her to do a reading."

Apparently more than happy to duck the glares of both his daughter and wife, Drake disappeared toward the kitchen, phone already in-hand.

"Why do you want Sybil to read right now?" she asked her mother.

Rue came closer and pointed at the chair nearest Liam's couch. "Cyan, give me some space."

Liam actually whimpered. "Oh, God, what now?"

Cyan tilted her head and glared at her mother.

Rue rolled her gray eyes. "I'm not going to hurt him. I just want to talk to him. Now, get out of my way."

Begrudgingly, Cyan let go of Liam and sat on the edge of a white, cushioned chair watching her mother sit on the coffee table, facing Liam, who—with his dark hair sticking up in sweaty points—closely resembled a small boy about to be punished.

"Don't look at me like I'm gonna bite."

"No offense, but you look like you might."

Cyan hid a smile behind her hand.

Rue folded her thin hands in her lap. "You said your parents died when you were very young. How did they die?"

"My mother died of cancer and my father, heart disease."

"Heart disease."

"Some said it was a broken heart."

Rue's right eye crinkled. "What about the rest of your family?"

"I don't have any."

"Aunts, uncles, cousins?"

He shook his head and coughed. "Nobody."

"Irish."

"What?"

"You're Irish," Rue said.

"Yes."

Cyan watched her mother stare at Liam. He stared back… before shuddering and falling back into the couch, clutching his stomach and chest. When Cyan moved to stand, Rue's upheld hand stopped her along with a shake of her head, a refusal.

"If I'm under a spell," he gasped, "what is it? Am I dying?"

"No."

Cyan jumped at the sound of her father's voice, right behind her.

Rue gazed at her husband. "You don't know that."

"Woman, come here," Drake commanded. He rarely used that voice, and even Cyan winced at memories of being in trouble as a little girl.

While her parents whispered, she slid from the chair and to the edge of the couch next to Liam's hip. She put her hand on his head and told him to breathe. "I'm going to fix you."

"Just promise it doesn't involve a fork."

She shook her head at the silly man who'd been dragged into her world and moved her hand to the center of his chest. The fabric of his black button down felt warm and wet from sweat. She closed her eyes and focused on the beat of his heart, and again, something warm tumbled around her stomach. The feeling, the stirring of magic, was almost becoming familiar.

"Cyan?" said her father's voice.

"I can heal him."

"No," Rue said.

"Mother—"

"I said no. We don't even know what kind of spell he's under. Lord knows what could happen if she drags whatever poison is in his system into her own body, into her own soul. No, I won't—"

"Love of my life," Drake said quietly. "Have faith in our little girl. She's gonna need it."

Cyan knew her father didn't refer to this moment but to the War. Healing Liam would be nothing compared to threats she would soon face from the Dorcha. And Cyan was tough, after all—the Loach foretold. Pulling a spell from Liam's system was to be child's play in comparison with what was to come. She knew it, and so did her father, although Rue looked wary.

"Mother. Let me."

Rue took a slow, long inhale through her nose and crossed her thin arms. She did, however, nod ever so slightly.

Cyan looked back to Liam whose eyes were closed. The warmth in her stomach increased, although whether from magic or affection, she wasn't sure. She was, however, sure of one thing. "Alone," she said.

"What?" her father asked.

"Let me do this alone."

Cyan knew her mother wanted to fight—she could sense her tension from across the living room—yet, Drake took his wife's hand and pulled her toward the front door. "Sybil's on her way. We'll get her some hot chocolate while you take care of him."

Cyan nodded in thanks as her parents vacated the area.

As the magic took over, she lost some control of herself, but she allowed the warmth to spread out from her stomach and into her arms and legs. She did as her body bid, straddling Liam on the couch. That's when he woke from his spell-induced stupor and his feverish green eyes stared up at her. "Cyan …"

"I'm gonna fix you."

He blinked in response.

Cyan leaned forward and unbuttoned his shirt. She pushed the fabric back from his bare chest, lean and hot to the touch. She laid her palms softly against his collarbone and focused—and felt nothing. She moved her hands lower, over his chest, and paused. By then, the warmth had spread to between her legs.

She looked up into his eyes, guilty, as though he might be able to see her unfamiliar arousal. Unmoving, he watched her. "Okay?" she asked.

His voice sounded gravelly. "Well, you haven't stabbed me with a magic fork yet."

She didn't smile because the palm of her right hand suddenly pulsed as if all the blood in her body might explode out her fist. She gasped through parted lips.

"Cyan?"

"It's in your heart," she said. "The spell is in your heart."

His chest rose and fell with breath beneath her.

"Don't move." She folded her hands together and rested them over his chest. She muttered the beginnings of a few incantations but found she didn't need them. Merely touching him, feeling Liam between her legs, was enough to make her hands burn—and apparently, they truly did burn, because Liam let out a shout as the morning light of sunrise was overtaken by a glittering gold that surrounded them both and filled the room. This was not like the blue light she had emitted previously. Neither did the expenditure of power weaken her, as it had at Sea Books. Instead, as she dislodged the spell from Liam's chest, her heart beat faster. Her body tingled.

He moaned beneath her—a not altogether unpleasant noise—as her hands pulled a rolling black cloud from his chest that rose, surrounding them, until it hit the ceiling and dispersed. With the spell's exorcism, the gold light dwindled from Cyan's hands.

Her body crumpled down on top of Liam's, not from exhaustion, but from the need to hold his body to hers. She panted against his throat and barely registered her own surprise as he wrapped his arms around her. He grabbed a handful of her thick braids and lifted her head enough to press his lips to hers. Unlike the kiss they'd shared in Sea Books, Liam was responsive this time; in fact, he was aggressive. He opened her mouth with his tongue, which made her entire body boil, and she moaned as he rolled to his side, pinning her to the back of the couch. Cyan wrapped her leg around him and pulled him closer with her hand on his lower back. He held tight to her ass and rutted against her until she felt a hardness against her upper thigh.

This realization—and her momentary pause in movement—must have restarted Liam's rational synapses because he stopped groping her with so much vigor that he fell off the couch and scooted away like a backwards-moving crab.

"I'm sorry. I'm so sorry."

She shook her head. "It was a side effect of the spell," she said, which was half true; the Craft *did* put her body into a state of excitement, even when she crashed after—but Liam's body carried similar consequence. "It's nothing, Liam. Do you feel okay? Better?"

He looked at the floor, seemingly assessing himself. "Yeah."

Cyan stood and pulled at her clothes, all of which were in a state of disarray. "Look, why don't you shower?"

He looked up at her, eyes wide.

"I mean, I'm going to leave. Give you some space. My mother will want to come check on you. Later. And we'll talk to Max, of course. He should be at the Bistro?"

Liam nodded and wiped his hand across his mouth.

"It was just the spell, Liam," she said. "You didn't dishonor Zoe."

He took a slow breath. "That was intense."

"Well, I'm going."

He grabbed her hand as she passed. "Thank you."

In the hallway outside his apartment, Cyan leaned her forehead against the wall and closed her eyes. Places on her body burned where his hands had touched her, and she tasted him on her mouth like dark red wine.

Chapter Thirteen

Liam took a guilty shower, scrubbing until his skin felt raw. He didn't scrub away the memory of Cyan as if she was something dirty—but what he'd done, the way he'd reacted… God, Zoe wasn't even in the ground. What the hell had gotten into him? Cyan blamed the spell, of course, but was what he felt just a spell? No, he knew it wasn't. He'd been physically attracted to Cyan before he even knew her name, when she was just "Blondie," according to the guys at the Bistro. And she was attracted to him, that much was obvious.

Cyan Burroughs might be strong enough to smash him into pavement. She might have supernatural abilities that belonged in the realm of fiction. Yet, he knew she was inexperienced with men. The careful way she touched him, the way her pale cheeks burned pink when he looked at her, and the pliant melting of her body against his on the couch: she'd never had sex. She didn't know what to do with Liam, but he knew what to do with her.

Nothing.

Whatever attraction existed between them, he would stop out of respect for Zoe. He would dissuade Cyan's infatuation—all business from here on out.

He shaved a bit ruthlessly, cutting himself once with the straight razor, and brushed his teeth twice. He picked out a black suit with a black button-down like a Victorian wife in mourning and stepped out of the bedroom, but as he did, the front door to the condo opened. Zoe walked in.

She was wearing a white summer dress, too thin for the weather outside. Her hair was in a high ponytail, and she must have been in a rush when she left the house that morning, because she'd only had time to apply a touch of mascara and blush. In her arms, she held paper bags of groceries. He spotted the top of a French baguette as she disappeared into the kitchen. She smiled when she saw him.

"Zoe." He moved to follow her but was forced to one knee as pain shot through his brow. He crouched and held to his forehead. The pain was so great, he was unable to scream but ended up on hands and knees, struggling to breathe.

When the searing—but now familiar—pain passed, he sat up to find the kitchen silent and empty. He checked. No bags of groceries from their local market. No Zoe.

Liam vacated the area immediately and headed straight to Broad Street. Crisp and cold, the salt-scented harbor air rifled through his short hair. Thick, oily gardenia leaves shifted in the breeze as he passed. The white blossoms remained, soon to disappear for the season, but he didn't smell their sweet perfume. He turned left onto Broad Street, almost empty of cars but haunted by memories of smoke and fire.

When he walked through the huge, glass front doors of Broad Street Bistro, the dining room was empty but already smelled of browned butter. The sound of a new arrival must have brought Tommy forth from the back kitchen. The squat sous chef dropped a towel when he saw Liam.

"Dude," he said. "What are you doing here?"

"I need to see Max."

Tommy shook his head. "I'm so sorry about your girl."

"Is he here?"

"No, uh, no one's seen him since yesterday afternoon." Tommy waved toward the darkened bar. "Can I get you a drink? I'll have one with you, man."

"Did Max call in last night? Why wasn't he here?"

Tommy shrugged. "I don't know. He's the owner. I guess he kinda does what he wants, you know?"

"Right. Okay." He looked back toward the palm trees outside.

"Liam. Is there anything I can do?"

He turned back toward Tommy who, for some reason, looked afraid. "Yeah. There is. Call me when Max shows up. I need to talk to him."

Tommy nodded. "You got it."

"Thanks." Liam turned to leave.

"I'm sorry," Tommy said again.

"Me, too." Liam shoved out the front door of the Bistro into the rising sun of Broad and almost ran into a skinny blonde woman wearing too much jewelry. "Rue."

"Liam," she squeaked—highly out of character for a woman who, in his experience, communicated via shout or scary ultimatum.

"What are you doing here?" he asked.

She had her daughter's eyes, and he found they studied him in the same way. "You look different."

He glanced down at his impeccable suit. "This is what I look like when I'm not… dying."

"You were never dying."

"Well."

"Is he here?" She nodded toward the entrance.

"No."

"You shouldn't have come here alone."

Liam squeezed his eyes shut and tried to calm down. "You know, I'm really sick of you people telling me what to do."

"Are you?" She crossed her arms, and he recognized that tone: the condescending one she usually reserved for Cyan.

"Yes," he hissed, moving closer so as to not alert the entire street of his rage that was rising like the tide. "You keep reminding me that I'm not of your world. Well, a witch caused the death of the woman I love and then almost killed me, possibly because of some mysterious involvement I have with your daughter. I *am* a part of your world now, and if you think I'm going to sit back and let you hunt the son of a bitch who destroyed my life alone, then you're…"

"Fine," she interrupted with a sniff, one nostril quirking up in what could only be described as a nasal sneer. "Come with me."

She spun on her bare foot and walked back down Broad. Her feet slapped the pavement as she went, but her lack of shoes did not detract from her hugely intimidating demeanor as she led him straight to Sea Books and shoved him inside.

The aunt, Sybil, jumped when she saw him. "Hell's bells, boy, you're something fine to look at this morning."

Rue huffed as she passed. "He's one of us. For now."

"What?" Sybil pulled a ratty shawl tight around her shoulders.

"If someone caused my death, would you let somebody else clean it up?"

Sybil blinked. "I'm pretty sure Drake would take care of that, darling."

"You get my meaning. Now, get your crystal ball. I want you to read him." She dragged Liam by his arm to behind the midnight blue curtain.

"Read me?"

She pulled him deeper into the store than he'd ever been before to a small, circular room with a table in the center and a smattering of chairs. "Yes." She shoved him into a chair. "You. I have some suspicions about you, boy."

"Guilty. I sometimes steal bottles of wine from work."

Rue shook her head. "Always gotta be funny."

"It's a defense mechanism," he said.

Sybil returned with a big, black box that unlocked at the top. It sounded like she wore tiny bells on her ankles as she moved around the table. She set the box down, muttered to herself, and lifted the box. What remained in its absence was a small purple crystal ball on a silver pedestal.

"It's made of amethyst, dear," Sybil said. "Stimulates the mind. The Plainacher family heirloom sphere was lost, so I had to make do."

She sat across from him and started muttering again as Rue pulled up a chair to his left and whispered her own words.

Amidst their whispers, though, Liam heard something else: sounds like children's voices. He glanced around the dusty, dark room but saw no little ones hiding in corners. Then, he realized the sound came from the crystal ball. He leaned closer and tilted his head, and the voices only increased. With one finger he reached out and brushed the surface of the sphere. A blue spark flew from his finger to the crystal orb, and the lilac purple amethyst changed and turned to swirling, soft clouds of blue.

The change in ambiance made Rue and Sybil's eyes pop open. Rue gasped, but Sybil giggled as she held her hand above the ball.

Liam held his hands against his chest. "Oh, my God, did I break it?"

Sybil looked up at him, head tilted. "Where'd you say you were from, Liam?"

"Ireland," Rue said, watching the crystal ball's hypnotic display of blue upon blue. "He's from Ireland. Haven't you heard him talk?"

"Why does it matter where I'm from?"

"Many of our people came from your country, child," Sybil said.

He stood and almost knocked the chair down. "Look, we need to find Max. How do we find Max?"

Instead of responding, Rue stood and took hold of Liam's face. She was a bit shorter than him, so she had to tilt his chin down to stare into his eyes. She studied him as one might study a newly discovered species. After an awkward amount of silence, she finally gave his cheek a gentle slap. "You have very nice eyes. Scrying mirror!"

"Huh?" he asked.

He followed Rue back toward the front of the shop. Behind him, Sybil moved, too, looking for something. He watched Cyan's mother reach for a small bowl. Then, she traveled around the back shelves of Sea Books, opening jars.

Liam stood over her. "Are you preparing a spice rub?"

She, surprisingly, chuckled. "I'm working a spell, Liam."

"With herbs?"

"Yes. Herbs are a very large part of what we do."

"I've never seen Cyan—"

"She's different. My specialty is potions, and I'm very good with a scrying mirror."

"Right, what is that?"

She grabbed a pestle and crushed the contents of the small bowl. "It allows me to see people, locate them. Hopefully, it'll lead us to Max."

"Is that how you found me? When I was ill?"

"Yes. Apologies for invading your personal space. I was looking for my daughter at the time."

"If you were looking for her, why did you find me?"

She threw a few more crushed herbs into the bowl. "I thought she might be with you."

"I don't think I understand."

Rue sighed. "Cyan doesn't show up in the mirror. She wears a very old pendant, passed down from the Plainacher family line that protects her, some, but not enough for me to sleep well at night." She stopped in her work and turned to face him, one hand on her hip. "My daughter is very important to my people."

"She told me about the prophecy."

"Did she, now?"

"I was half conscious at the time. Maybe she thought I'd forget."

"Mm." She turned back to her work.

"Do you really believe Cyan could *kill* this… dark witch person?"

Rue sighed. "If it's kill or be killed, I believe so. And if it's to save the world from endless darkness, what wouldn't you do?"

"If Max is behind this, I'll kill him just for hurting Zoe."

Rue nodded. "I wasn't sure about you at first, but I like the way you think."

Sybil returned with a black mirror and set it on a book-strewn desk. Liam noticed there was no reflection in its surface, just deep black like the bottom of the sea. Rue set the bowl of herbs in front of it and whispered words he now recognized were Gaelic—from his island, as it were.

"Max's full name?" she said.

"Henny. Max Henny."

Liam noticed Max's name mixed with the rest of the incantations. He stood and waited until the mirror started to shift. Shapes like storm clouds moved within its depths, but just as a streak of light began to show, the mirror went black again.

Rue blew out a loud breath. "Well, he's definitely a witch, and a powerful one at that. I can't see a damn thing because he's shrouded himself."

"Probably knows we're looking," Sybil said.

"A guy I work with," Liam said, "he's going to call if Max shows up at the Bistro, but he hasn't been there since yesterday."

"Maybe he's running," Rue said.

"Not if he's after Cyan. Or me. I'm sure you were hoping I'd forget what your husband said, about Cyan and I being connected. What did he mean?"

Rue laughed and shook her head. "That is another story for another day, boy. Right now, I need a strong cup of tea." She walked through the midnight blue curtain.

A small hand wove gently into Liam's, and he looked down to see Sybil smiling up at him.

"You see all these things in this room," she whispered. She waved her arm, covered in gold bangles, toward the ceiling where different stones, gems, and mirrors hung from silver strings. "They're for protection against anyone who'd want to do harm. They're not as powerful as Cyan's pendant, but if you ever feel like you're in danger, you come here, and you'll be safe."

"Why would I be in danger?"

She smiled some more, but the expression didn't reach her eyes. "Magic can be very dark, Liam. It can do very bad things in the wrong hands. But it can save people and be beautiful, too. You wanna see something beautiful, sweetheart?"

He inclined his head toward her.

She said something that sounded like "Lamprog," waved her hand, and the entire room lit up with floating, pink fireflies. Liam laughed, his eyes watering at the dreamscape before him. He held his hand out, and one of the glowing bugs landed on the tip of his finger. It faltered and buzzed before floating back toward the ceiling, emitting a trail of pink glitter in its wake.

"Amazing."

Sybil reached up and wiped a tear from his cheek he hadn't even noticed was there.

Chapter Fourteen

Cyan beat the hell out of a punching bag at the gym. Even though her hands were wrapped, after a half hour of attack, she fell to the floor and felt them ache. "Damn it," she muttered. It wasn't anger she channeled into the bag; it was tension, of the sexual variety. "This is why you weren't supposed to show up yet," she said to no one, although a guy nearby did turn to look at her.

Her glare made him look away.

Finding Liam now, under these circumstances, had been exactly what Cyan did not want. She wanted to eventually meet the man who would love her—even if, according to Sybil, they might not have a happy ending—but not until after the War so that she wouldn't be distracted by his emerald green eyes or the way his lips quirked and his eyebrows rose when he was amused. Or the way he smelled like cologne and oak barrels.

She huffed out a growl and stood, taking one bare-knuckled heave at the huge punching bag that trembled beneath her touch.

This was not the time to think about Liam's abs.

As her mother had so eloquently put the night before, Cyan stank, so she took a long shower at the gym before stepping out into a chilled but sunny Charleston afternoon. The sky was the color of the blue glow her skin gave off whenever Liam touched her—which made her wonder why her magic had glowed gold that morning. Was it possible for a witch's magic to manifest in two colors? She'd never heard of such a thing, but she was the Loach, after all. She supposed anything was possible.

Cyan wandered away from her gym toward her tiny apartment that overlooked East Bay. The entrance door was squeezed between two bars that would be hopping with the lunch crowd soon enough. She stomped up the steps to her apartment, suddenly exhausted, and found her father inside already, sitting on her couch, spinning his pocket-knife.

She closed the door with her boot. "I believe they call this invasion of privacy."

"Your mother would say you're my child, so you don't deserve privacy."

She snorted. Her apartment was half the size of Liam's. She'd lived there for three years but never gotten around to decorating, so the space was perpetually empty of character. She rarely used her bed in the back room, opting more often to curl up on the couch—a hand-me-down from her parents' basement. Her kitchen was covered in books on the Craft that pride told her she no longer needed and there wasn't a scrap of food in the joint, which was possibly why her daddy looked perturbed.

"How was your workout?"

"Good, except I bruised the hell out of—" She looked down at her fists. "Huh. Apparently, I'm subconsciously healing myself now."

"That's why I'm here, little girl."

"I suppose so."

Drake leaned forward on the couch, wearing his usual stylistic choice of plaid flannel and dark jeans with big, brown boots. "How'd you feel after you healed Liam this morning?"

She blushed in response.

He smiled like he knew. "Nothing to be embarrassed about."

"I felt fine." She reached for a water bottle from the fridge. "Not like before. I wasn't weakened by using magic this time."

"Good. That's the last thing we'll need in battle. You passing out every time you cast."

"Speaking of battle, did you find Max?"

Drake shook his head. "He high-tailed it. Not sure why or how he knew we were onto him. Then again, if he is the Dorcha, he's probably been one step ahead of us this whole time."

"Shit, shouldn't someone be keeping an eye on Liam? What if—"

"I wouldn't worry about him right now. We gotta focus on you."

She nodded. "I know."

Her daddy stood and tucked his pocketknife away. "What's it been feeling like when you do these spells?"

"Warm. Really warm. And like something's twisting in my stomach. Nothing bad." She paused. "Kind of like a good Bloody Mary."

Father and daughter shared a smile.

"My light was gold this morning, Daddy, not blue like the other times. You ever heard of that happening?"

"You're the Loach, little girl. I don't know what might happen to you, what you might become." He appeared to have trouble swallowing. "You're about to become stronger than all of us, that's for sure, which is why you need to learn to control it—the anger part at least. I'd say that's our most pressing issue. We can't have you hurting anyone accidentally, especially your mother, since she's the person on this Earth who pisses you off the most."

"Yeah."

"You also can't be tied to Liam for your powers. You got to be able to do this on your own, although, way I figure, he can be your focus—carry a picture of him in your head and project your spells through that image of him. I think they'll carry more power."

She leaned against the kitchen counter. "Why did he have to show up right now, with all this going on?"

"Destiny has no respect for timing, but we'll keep him out of the line of fire."

"So you think this Max guy knows about Sybil's visions, my connection to Liam? Jesus, do you think that's why he got the job at the Bistro, like, maybe Max recognized him and hired him on the spot?"

Drake put his hands on his hips, considering. "It's a possibility."

"But he couldn't know about me!" She clutched the pendant around her neck. "Grandmother's amulet protects me. Even a powerful witch can't see me for what I am."

"It doesn't shield Sybil. Or your mother."

Cyan sighed.

"Or me. If Max has a scrying mirror, he could be watching us right now."

"Fuck."

"Fuck, indeed. There aren't enough spells to hide us all from the likes of the Dorcha, not even all the shit your aunt hangs up in her store or the spells surrounding our house. Those spells will protect us, but he can still *see* us."

She started to speak.

"Yes, even when I'm invisible. I won't be invisible to him, so I'm counting on you."

She nodded. "Well. Then, let's get some work done."

They spent the afternoon hurling spells at each other, some of which sent Cyan flying backwards into walls and left her choking for breath. However, Drake took similar beatings, which pleased her since her daddy was the human equivalent of Bigfoot. Just like that morning, the light that pulsed from Cyan's palms was glittery-gold like the hair of some fairytale princess. Her father's murky gray lacked in showmanship but made up for that in power. Drake Burroughs was not a man to trifle with, and as the day wore on, Cyan realized she was not a woman to be trifled with either. She hooted when her daddy's body broke the one piece of furniture she'd actually bought: an antique table by the window overlooking East Bay.

Drake cussed. "I'm too old for this shit."

She fought to pull her father's hulking figure up off the floor—not an easy task. "Then, let's quit for the day and go have a drink."

"Your mother's making dinner."

"To the homestead, then. Let's go."

He brushed himself off. "Sounds mighty fine. Oh, and dinner involves a guest."

"A guest?"

Drake cleared his throat. "Come on. I want a beer. Maybe several." He tilted his head back and forth until his neck cracked.

They walked together through the dwindling light of downtown Charleston. The gas lamps hissed and burned gold on street corners. Dark green ivy reached out like fingers fighting for ankles. Instead of talking, Drake whistled.

"What is that, some Disney nonsense?"

"What? No. It's *Les Miserables*. 'On My Own.' Didn't I teach you anything?"

"Yeah, how to drink."

He elbowed her playfully.

"Who's this guest for dinner?"

Drake sighed just as their house came into view—light blue and painted in layers of ivy with slowly dying white blooms. Potted plants covered the front porch as her father kept walking and opened the front door.

She heard her mother's voice: "I've been making eggplant Parmesan since you were pissing in a diaper."

A man's voice said, "Well, then, you've been doing it wrong for a very long time. No, stop. Give me—"

Cyan froze in the foyer that smelled of tomatoes and garlic. "What is Liam doing here?"

"Ask your mother."

She watched her father walk away before following quickly behind.

Liam and Rue stood at the huge kitchen island with a cutting board full of sliced eggplant in front of them. Liam wore black trousers and a black button down, covered in an embarrassingly frilly light green apron, and held a mound of salt in his palm. "Look, if you salt eggplant before cooking it and let it sit, the salt draws the bitter liquid out.

After a half hour, we pat the pieces dry and put together our casserole. That way, the eggplant won't be soggy."

Rue groaned. "Not only am I taking advice from a child but a *male* child. This is humiliating."

Liam smiled as he spread salt over the waiting eggplant. Cyan almost fainted when she noticed Rue smiling, too.

"Mother?"

Rue and Liam's heads popped up. "Cyan. How'd it go today?"

Drake grabbed a beer from the fridge and threw one to his daughter. Cyan caught it. She didn't usually drink beer, but right then, she wanted a beer and then some. "Fine. Liam." She tilted her head.

He opened his mouth but no sound came out. He closed and opened it again. "Your mom invited me for dinner."

"We've spent the whole day together." Rue put her hand on Liam's shoulder. "He was very helpful around the shop actually."

"*Mother*." She squeezed the word out through tight lips. "Can I talk to you for a second?" Without waiting for a response, she walked into the den where Drake did his reading and spent the occasional afternoon watching horse races on TV.

Perceptively, Rue closed the door behind her.

"Why did you spend the day with Liam?"

"I ran into him at Bistro, where he went *alone* looking for Max, stupid boy. Made me realize someone needs to keep an eye on him, while you need to be focusing on the Craft."

"So, what, you're his babysitter now?"

Rue pursed her lips and looked at the ceiling like a child being punished for something small and silly. "After today, I'll keep an eye from a distance, but he… something's the matter with him."

"Yes, the woman he loves is dead."

"I think his parents were witches."

"What?"

Rue glanced over her shoulder. "Oh, keep your voice down. He's an orphan from Ireland—the land of our people's history. You think that's a coincidence?"

"Uh, which part? Dead parents or the Emerald Isle?"

"Don't be smart with me."

"I'm not being smart, Mother. Are you saying you think Liam is a witch?"

"He touched Sybil's crystal ball this morning, and it turned blue." Rue shrugged.

"Blue."

"Yeah."

Cyan set her beer on her father's desk. "I've seen blue light come off him before. It's happened twice, but only when we were touching. I thought it was my light, but after today, we've pretty much confirmed my light is gold. Daddy said, being the Loach and all, I could have two colors, but…" She shook her head. "What if the blue light is Liam?"

"He could come from witches and not even know it."

"Being near Liam makes me feel more powerful. What if Max knows that, and he was trying to kill Liam in the accident and not someone on the trolley, like we thought?"

"Oh, bless me," Rue said. "Well, we can't let that boy out of our sight."

Liam's voice called from the kitchen. "Hey, Queen of the Kitchen, come help put this casserole together!"

Cyan grabbed her mother's arm. "How are we going to tell him? I don't know how much more he can take. He lost Zoe. Then, a witch tried to poison him, a witch who turned out to be one of his only friends in Charleston. He's gonna flip."

Rue nodded slowly. "Okay, the epiphany can wait. For now, you call Sybil. Tell her to go to his condo and do the full gamut of protective spells while he's here with us. He won't even know she's done a thing. Tell her to keep out anyone who means him harm."

Cyan nodded and did as she was told. After she hung up, she stood there listening to Liam laugh and the deep chuckle of her own daddy in response. It seemed the War just got a lot more complicated.

Chapter Fifteen

Although the night was cold, Liam didn't feel it, not because he was warm on familial comfort but because he didn't feel anything. He held a steaming cup of tea in his palms and sat on the back porch of the Burroughs homestead. He stared into the shadows of the night garden and took a long, shaky breath.

"Liam?"

Over his shoulder, Cyan lingered in the doorway. Her white-blonde hair glowed from the light pouring forth from the hallway that led to the kitchen, where the family had just consumed Liam's eggplant Parmesan—and agreed it was the best they'd ever had. She took a few sure-footed steps forward and sat next to him, keeping at least a foot between them. Ever since the incident on his couch that morning, she'd been keeping her distance, even sitting all the way across from him at the dinner table.

"Zoe was very fond of that dish." He ran his thumb up and down the outside of the scalding cup.

Cyan didn't say anything. She wrapped her arms around herself, clad again in her familiar leather jacket.

"She couldn't cook," he said. "It was an absolute disaster every time she went into the kitchen."

"Did you try to teach her?"

"No. I just cooked for her instead. I like cooking."

"Never heard that from a guy before."

Liam took a sip of tea; it tasted of mint. "Drake not much of a chef?"

"Daddy can make macaroni and cheese. Out of the box." She stretched her legs in front of her, heavy combat boots resting in the grass.

"How long have your parents been married?"

"Twenty-eight years. I think. Something like that."

"I don't remember my parents."

She tilted her head toward him until some of her long braids fell over her shoulder. "You don't remember anything about them? Even from before boarding school?"

He chuckled. "You make it sound so tragic. I'm not Oliver Twist, Cyan. I'm a trust fund brat. I have more money than I've ever needed. I've never wanted for anything—except companionship, I suppose."

"So you're a rich bitch," she said, not cruelly.

"Little good it's ever done me." He took another sip of tea.

"Why do you work? Why don't you just travel around being rich?"

He shrugged. "It's never felt like my money. It's the money of dead strangers."

"You consider your parents strangers?"

He bit down on his bottom lip and stared into the garden where shadows gave way to black. "I have one memory of my mother in a hospital bed. She looked so sick. So sad. I remember she kept holding my hand."

"No mother wants to leave her child." She glanced back at the house. "Except maybe mine."

Liam shook his head. "Rue loves you. She's just tough. Kinda scary tough, really."

"Yeah."

He held tightly to the mug in his hands. "Zoe liked tea. She couldn't stand if I had coffee breath in the morning. Something odd: I can't remember how she tastes. Her lips. Isn't that odd?"

Cyan put her hand on his forearm.

"How can I be forgetting her already? It just fucking happened."

"You've been through a lot since it happened."

"I saw her this morning. In our kitchen. Bringing home bags of groceries."

Cyan's hand held tighter to his arm.

"Seeing her this morning… all this…" He waved back toward the house. "I feel like I've gone crazy."

Cyan scooted a little closer. "You're not crazy."

"Maybe you're just a pretty hallucination."

"You think I'm pretty?"

He sighed and closed his eyes, so he didn't notice how close Cyan was until he felt her thigh along the side of his and her hands on his face. She dipped low and caught his lips in a hard, smoldering kiss that pushed roughly against his mouth as she clung to the back of his head. His eyes shot open, but there was no light passing between them. There was no use of the Craft here. She kissed him because she wanted to—desperately, based on the way she sucked at his bottom lip—which made him pull back and shove her away with such force that he dropped the teacup. It shattered at his feet as he stood.

"What the—?" He ran his hands through his hair and turned away from her. He bellowed into the garden, the cry of an enraged animal. He spun back around and glared down at Cyan who looked up at him with a mix of anger and fear. "I shouldn't be here with you, not like this. I don't even know you or your family," he said, just in time for Rue and Drake to come rushing outside at the sound of his cries.

"What's going on?" Rue asked.

"I made a mistake." Cyan curled her arms around her knees and stared at the ground.

Drake put his hands on his wife's shoulders. "What kind of mistake?"

Liam shook his head. "It doesn't matter. I have to go."

"You can't." He would swear Rue's gray eyes were glowing.

"Like hell I can't."

"Not on your own. Drake will have to walk you."

Liam's mouth hung open. "What am I, a goddamn five year old?"

"No," Rue said. She glanced at her daughter. "You're a witch, and you need our protection."

He laughed into the night. "A witch? Me. No, you're crazy."

"You think you got pulled into all this by accident, boy?"

He shook his head. "You're wrong." His chest felt tight. "There's nothing magical about me, nothing special. Furthermore, if I was a witch, wouldn't I have saved the woman I love? Instead, she's dead because of *your* people. I had nothing to do with it."

Calmly, Rue said, "Look at your hands."

"What?"

"Look at your hands, Liam," Cyan whispered.

He lifted his hands and found his palms glowing a deep shade of blue. "Wha—" His hands shook, and the light throbbed brighter, darker, brighter. The world went fuzzy around the edges.

"He's going down," Drake said just as Liam's knees crumbled. He felt the other man's strong arm around his shoulders but was not thankful for it because at that moment he wanted nothing more than to bang his head against the steps and wake from this horrible dream.

He and Drake ended up sitting on the ground. Liam's hands had stopped glowing, but he couldn't stop staring at them. *Traitors.*

Rue knelt in front of him and lifted his chin so he was looking at her. "You ready to be sensible now?"

"Are you fucking kidding me?"

Beside him, Drake chuckled.

"How long have you known?" Liam asked.

"Known?" Rue shook her head. "I *suspected* when you touched Sybil's crystal ball. Now, I know."

"My parents?"

Rue nodded. "Were witches, I assume, but they died before they could tell you about it."

"My mother died of cancer. Couldn't my father have fixed her?"

Rue looked up at her husband, who said, "You can't fix everything with light magic. Dark magic, perhaps, but no one enters that territory without some serious consequences. Trust me."

Cyan still remained on the back steps, arms folded around herself, looking anywhere but at him. "I'm sorry I yelled at you, Cyan."

She gave a quick shake of her head as if to erase the way she'd kissed him before.

"And about your teacup," he told Rue.

She smiled and shook her head. "You are one polite young man."

"You said I need your protection. Why?"

There was a collective trading of glances between the three Burroughs kin like arrows going back and forth.

"Please," he begged. "Just tell me what's going on."

Rue spoke, cold and precise. "We think the trolley accident was intended to kill you."

"Oh," he said. "Because Max knows I'm a witch?"

Rue nodded slowly.

"But I didn't even know I was a witch until…" He held up his hands and shook them.

"If Max is as powerful as we expect, if he is the Dorcha, he probably knew about you before we did. He might have known as soon as you set foot in Charleston."

"He gave me the job at the Bistro."

"Maybe to keep you close," Rue said. "Keep an eye on you until he was ready to attack."

Drake looked up at the stars. "He would have wanted it to be a spectacle, to get our attention. Possibly the attention of the whole Craft community in Charleston."

"The Dorcha's coming out party," Cyan muttered.

Liam pointed at Cyan. "She's the super witch, the…"

"Loach," Cyan said.

"I'm nobody."

"From what we've observed, you increase her power. Maybe Max expected as much, what with Sybil's—" Rue stopped talking.

"Just tell him about the paintings, Mother."

Nobody spoke, and a moment later, the only sound was the ringing of Liam's cell phone. He pulled it from his pocket and glanced at the caller ID. "It's the hospital. This is Liam Cody," he answered and, moments later, started screaming into the phone.

He didn't complain when the entire Burroughs family followed him to Charleston Memorial Hospital. They were a mismatched group, Liam in a suit, Cyan in leather, Rue in hippie skirts, and Drake in a stained canvas jacket.

Outside the morgue, he got right in the police officer's thick, chiseled face. "What do you mean, her body's been stolen?"

"Sir, we didn't say stolen. We said missing."

He lowered his voice from scream to murderous whisper. "How does a dead body go missing?"

"Well, that's why we're here: to find out. I would ask you to calm down please."

"Calm down?" He laughed something damn near hysterical. "The hospital lost my girlfriend's body. Why would I be calm?"

Cyan, whom he hadn't even noticed standing right next to him, grabbed him by the wrist, dragged him backwards, and shoved him around a corner and against a wall. "Look at me."

He looked at her.

"Look at your hands."

They burned blue. "Shit."

She covered his hands with hers, small yet powerful. "Liam, breathe."

He took a breath in through his nose, out through his mouth. He leaned his forehead against hers and let the tears come until his chest shook with the deep anguish and fear that pumped through every cell in his body. When his hands warmed, he looked down to see Cyan's gold light enveloping his blue, embracing it until it disappeared. She wrapped her arms around him and let him sob against the collar of her coat, just as he had the night of the accident—a night that felt like eons ago.

"I've gone mad. That's it. I've gone completely mad. I'm in a padded cell somewhere, yeah?"

She shook her head against his. "This is all very real."

"What if I don't want it? What if I don't want any of this… this magic?"

She pulled away and looked up at him. Her eyes were sad pools deep enough for drowning. "You don't have a choice. None of us do. But I will keep you safe. I promise."

"Why would you do that for me?"

She tilted her head down and spoke to his chest. "Because I've loved you my whole life."

He would have perhaps given that statement some thought if not for the scalding pain behind his eyes. Then, the world went dark.

Chapter Sixteen

Luckily, Liam only passed out long enough for Cyan to catch him, heal him, and get him the hell out of there.

Back at the homestead, her father asked, "How's a dead body go missing?"

"And what's the meaning of these headaches?" Cyan added.

To help answer that question, Rue had Liam in their living room with her hand on his head while Drake, Sybil, and Cyan watched from behind the closed glass doors of Drake's den. Sybil was sitting in the leather desk chair, rocking back and forth, and Drake was holding onto the edge of the desk like he might break it in half.

"Maybe the headaches are his power waking up," Drake said, his voice uncharacteristically sharp and clipped.

"What's the matter with you?" Cyan asked.

"I'm a little worried about the missing corpse."

"Zoe. She had a name."

"Well, if a dark witch got ahold of her body, she won't be Zoe anymore—not the way he remembers." Drake nodded at Liam.

"Don't tell me," Cyan whispered.

"It's possible a dark witch could bring her body back to life, but her soul…" Drake shook his head.

"To what purpose?"

"Throw us off balance. Anyone messes with that boy now messes with you, and the Dorcha knows that."

"What if Liam's the Dorcha?" Cyan asked.

Like a movie set to pause, the room froze. Sybil stopped rocking in her chair, and Drake stood, mouth wide open, staring at Cyan.

"You said the headaches might be due to his power waking up. He didn't start getting those headaches until they moved here, to Charleston, close to me—which is about the time my powers started showing up, too."

Drake shook his head. "His eyes are green. I've checked. Both of 'em. Not one blue and one green. Just green, like St. Patty's Day."

"You said a powerful witch could hide his or her eye color."

Drake held his hand out, palm up, toward Liam and Rue in the living room. "The boy ain't a powerful witch. He doesn't know a single thing about the Craft. Also, let's not forget his earlier point about being able to save his woman if he was a witch. Instead, her corpse is floating around Charleston somewhere."

"He's your true love," Sybil said. "I know he is."

"Oh, fuck all that, Sybil. Who's to say my one true love wouldn't be bad?"

She shook her head, but Drake spoke before Sybil could retort. "If Liam is the Dorcha, he would have been prophesized. As a child in Ireland, someone would have known. He would have been raised, like you, to prepare for the War. He would have had a dark witch at his side from birth until now." Drake again gestured toward the living room. "That boy is alone. He doesn't have backup. There is no way he's the Dorcha. Max is the Dorcha."

"Fine." Cyan took a deep breath. "So what do we do with Liam until we find Max? Lock him in our basement?"

"Oh, it's very damp down there," Sybil said.

Cyan rolled her eyes. "I'm going for a walk."

"Where to?" Drake watched his wife and Liam. A soothing white glow lit the room as Rue used her magic.

"To see Grandmother. Maybe she'll have something to say this evening." She left the den, and both Rue and Liam looked up as Cyan walked to the liquor cabinet and pulled out a bottle of Grey Goose. "I'm going out."

"With vodka?" Rue paused knowingly. "Your grandmother drank whiskey."

Cyan harrumphed.

Liam tried to stand, but Rue kept her hand on his knee. "You're staying here, boy," she told him.

He sighed. "Be careful, Cyan."

"Don't worry about me."

Cyan enjoyed night walks—they tended to calm her down, especially when she went to visit Grandmother Plainacher's grave—but tonight the usual comfort of darkness felt oppressive. Taking long glugs of burning liquor, she walked away from the silent outskirts of downtown Charleston and in the direction of the center of the peninsula, Meeting Street. She passed crooked old plantation houses, painted bright shades of yellows and blues, colors dimmed in the moonlight. Using the hand not holding the rapidly emptying bottle, she ran her fingertips across black wrought iron fences as she walked, considering Liam, considering Zoe—whatever had become of her.

She turned onto Meeting and found the city quiet, only passing a few drunken parties on street corners. A homeless man played Bach on guitar, but she had no money to give him, and she wasn't about to share a shot. She kept walking until she spotted the high, rounded dome of St. Agnes and ducked beneath the limbs of Angel Oaks and webs of thick, Spanish moss to enter the cemetery. Her grandmother was waiting—her grand tombstone, at least—and Cyan took a seat in front of the grave, bottle between her legs, and stared at the name of her kin.

"You feel like talking tonight?" Cyan asked.

A bird cawed behind her, sounded like a crow.

"You know that boy I've been talking about my whole life? Well, someone's trying to get to me through him. Someone's messing up his life because of me—because of *destiny*." She sneered at the word. "This is your fault, you know. You didn't have to dub me the Loach while still in the womb. I couldn't fight back then, couldn't say you were wrong. Of course, I know you're not wrong. I can feel it, like a big, warm lump in my stomach." She paused. "And no, I'm not pregnant. You should know better." She took a sip of vodka as a small animal rustled nearby bushes. The air smelled of damp, green moss.

Someone walked up the sidewalk on Meeting Street—someone in high heels, which seemed a bit strange for that high up on Meeting at that time of night. Cyan glanced over her shoulder, hoping she wasn't going to have to help some lost, drunk girl home, but she didn't see anyone and turned back to her grandmother.

"We need to find Max. Do you know where he is?"

Her grandmother's tombstone was silent.

Cyan pulled at a piece of grass. "I know what the prophecy says, but do you really think I'm capable of killing someone?"

"Yes," a voice hissed from behind her, which made Cyan spin, backpedal, and leap behind her grandmother's tombstone. "Witchy, witchy, witch," the voice sang. The click of heels over uneven stone moved closer.

Cyan's hand went to the Plainacher black agate pendant around her neck.

"I know you're here," said a quiet, female voice. The woman laughed. "I smell him on you. He always smelled so good."

Cyan peered carefully over the edge of the tombstone. A curtain of Spanish moss parted, and Zoe, Liam's very dead beloved, stepped through. She didn't look like a character from a zombie flick; she looked like the picture on Liam's fridge: an attractive, dark-haired woman with pale skin and dark red lips. She wore a long, black trench coat, cinched tightly at the waist, and black pumps. She stood straight, and her dark eyes looked back and forth, up and down.

"That feels like a powerful amulet you wear." Zoe walked by the tombstone, close enough for Cyan to notice her fingernails, dark polish cracked from the accident. "What are you doing with him, anyway, you nervous virgin? You wouldn't know how to please a man like Liam." She scraped her hand across the top of an aged marble stone. "Do you look at him and get weak in the knees? Most women do. It's part of his charm, the way he looks. We make quite the fetching couple, Liam and I. Would you dare steal him from me?" Zoe ducked her head beneath a branch and spun around.

Cyan covered her mouth with her hand to stifle her rapid breath.

"I'm a very jealous woman, little witch. You won't have him, not now that I'm back." She paused and tilted her head. "Are you listening?" she whispered.

Cyan fought the urge to scream.

"Hey!" A man's voice echoed between rows of the dead. "What do you think you're doing here after dark?"

It took a moment for Cyan to realize she was being addressed—and Zoe was nowhere to be seen. As the man came closer, Cyan left the almost empty Grey Goose, got up, and ran. She sprinted back to her parents' home, never once looking over her shoulder. By the time she reached their front door, she was panting and practically drunk. She fell onto her knees in the foyer, legs quaking.

"What in God's name?" Rue held a teacup, as did Liam and Sybil, who sat on the couch.

"She's not dead," Cyan said.

Liam's teacup spilled as he set it down. He knelt in front of Cyan and took hold of her shoulders. She realized he *did* always smell good, which only made her shiver more.

"What happened?" he demanded.

Cyan looked up at him. "Zoe's not dead. I saw her."

"Your father said whoever stole her body could reanimate her," Rue said.

"What?" Liam shouted.

"No." Cyan shook her head. "It wasn't like that. She wasn't a walking corpse. She was the woman on Liam's fridge. Alive."

"I saw her this morning," he said, then shook his head. "But it wasn't real. It was just my imagination, and you've been drinking."

"This felt very real," Cyan said. "Where's Daddy?"

“Looking for answers. Looking for magic. Talking to some folks and trying to locate Max,” Rue said.

Sybil sat next to Cyan on the foyer floor, the fabric from her skirts pooling around her like a multi-colored cloud. She put her hand to Cyan’s forehead until Cyan’s whole head glowed pink. Used to her aunt’s magic, she didn’t move.

Sybil smiled. “The amulet. The amulet, it… Hmm.” She moved her hand from Cyan’s forehead to the heavy pendant at her throat. “She didn’t see you. You just saw her, isn’t that right, baby girl?”

Cyan nodded. “She knew I was there, though. She said she smelled Liam on me.”

Sybil nodded and put a hand on Liam’s shoulder. “You do smell lovely, dear.”

“I don’t understand what’s going on,” he said, and Cyan felt even worse for the guy, perpetually confused.

“Here’s my concern,” Sybil said slowly, still wearing a soft smile. “Grandmother’s amulet only protects Cyan from other witches.”

“You think his woman is a witch, too,” Rue said, arms crossed.

Sybil nodded.

“Okay, ignoring the complete insanity of that, Zoe is dead.” Liam pushed back on his heels until he fell to sitting on the foyer floor.

“Death is a…” Sybil wiggled her fingers. “Questionable state, young man, at least in the magical community.”

“So Zoe’s alive?”

“I did not say that either. However, that does not mean Cyan was not just in the presence of a ghost.”

Cyan waited for Liam to start screaming about the existence of ghosts. Instead, he said, calmly, “What time is it?”

Rue looked toward the clock in the kitchen. “Eleven.”

He nodded. “Cyan and I are going out for a drink.”

“But—” Rue started.

Cyan shook her head. “I’m in complete agreement. Sooner the better, in fact.”

"Girl, you are already two sheets to the wind."

"Let's go for three," she muttered.

She stayed close to Liam as they walked as if he could protect her—and maybe he could, from Zoe at least, even if she was only a ghost. On East Bay, Liam walked right past Pearlz without a moment's hesitation.

"Hey, let's go here," Cyan said.

"Smells too much like fish."

She took a few hurried steps to keep up with him and his six inches—at least—of extra height, although she almost tripped. The world had taken on a pleasant, fuzzy feeling. "You don't like seafood? But you live in Charleston," she muttered.

"Plus, their wine selection is shit, and I'm craving wine like a pregnant woman craves pickles." He wrapped his fingers around her forearm and tugged her forward. "Come on."

They ended up in a place Cyan never went: the Charleston Grill. It was too expensive for her tastes, and she didn't really look the part in her worn leather jacket, big boots, and bloodshot eyes. Liam fit in perfectly with his all-black suit, trimmed brown hair, and flawless skin. The hostess almost fell over her own feet on her way to them, but he waved her away and gestured to the bar.

Cyan followed behind, taking in the sight of marble floors and crystal chandeliers. Tables were covered in white cloths, candles, and plates with tiny pieces of decorative food. Waiters scurried about in long, black aprons while customers sipped wine from huge goblets or martinis from slim glasses. A jazz quartet played in the corner in front of a large photograph of a black woman singing. Cyan guessed she was supposed to recognize the woman but didn't.

She got some weird looks as she walked up to the bar, either due to her wild hair or vodka buzz, but she didn't care—not at the moment. Before Liam even saw the wine list, offered to him by a smiling female bartender, Cyan asked for a double shot of Grey Goose. She took it down in one gulp only to notice Liam watching her.

"What?"

"That can only end badly."

"Everything in my life ends badly."

He ordered a glass of something Cyan couldn't pronounce—sounded Italian. "You're talking about the War," he said. "What does the prophecy say? Are you supposed to die in this thing?"

She shrugged. "Maybe. Nobody knows. The last lines are kind of iffy. It's gonna be ugly, though." When the bartender brought Liam his glass of dark, red wine, Cyan gestured for more vodka.

"So other people might die," he said.

"Probably."

"That's why you're alone."

She glared at him.

"I'm sorry. I don't know why I said that." He wrapped his fingers around the tall wine glass stem. "I apologize."

She took a sip of booze. Even though she almost always drank Bloody Mary's, she liked straight vodka, too. The straight stuff was an emergency solvent, in her opinion, to be consumed in times of great travail, emotional or physical. "No, you're right. I am alone. I always have been, although I've never been the best company anyway."

"I like being around you."

"You're obviously a homicidal maniac."

He chuckled, and she turned to look at him. The hazy overhead light burnt delicately in a shade of gold—not as beautiful as Cyan's magic but enchanting nonetheless. Or perhaps it was the way the light touched the angles of Liam's face that made it seem so lovely. She noticed the bartender ogling him from the corner, and Cyan stared down at the floor, feeling oddly embarrassed as she wondered what that pretty bartender thought of her. Did she wonder what right Cyan had to sit next to a guy like Liam, little freak that she was?

"What did Zoe say when you saw her?" Liam asked, plucking her from her pity party.

She finished her shot of vodka and ordered another, head beginning to float dangerously. "She said I shouldn't… didn't deserve to be around you. She said I couldn't steal you away from her, that I wasn't good enough. Just a silly little virgin."

"That doesn't sound like Zoe."

"No?"

He shook his head. "She got jealous sometimes, but…"

The jazz quartet interrupted their silence.

Finally, armed with more liquor, Cyan said, "She didn't seem like a ghost. She seemed real."

"Well, Zoe wasn't a witch."

"How do you know?"

He chewed his bottom lip before answering. "I don't." He ran his hands through his hair, wine barely touched on the bar. "If she was a witch, why wasn't she a better cook?"

Cyan chortled, and Liam smiled.

"It's good to see you laugh," he said.

"It's good to see you smile."

"I should have taught her how to cook."

"I'm sure you taught her a couple things."

He leaned one elbow on the bar and looked at her. "Did you just make a sexual innuendo? We have to cut you off." He pretended to reach for her shot glass, but she smacked his hand away.

"Mine."

"Yes, ma'am."

She took another sip. The room looked filtered as though through a thick screen door. She noticed a woman passing the bar—a beautiful woman with long, black hair and rouged cheeks. The woman stared at Liam as she passed, and Cyan felt an ugly sting in her chest.

"Women find you very attractive, don't they?" she asked.

"Why did that sound like an accusation?"

"Well, it's true. You've never had any difficulty in that department, have you?"

"Okay." He reached for his wallet. "I think it's time we got you back home."

"We're just having a conversation."

"That's not how it feels." He gestured to the bartender.

"All these women in here are wondering why the fuck I'm sitting next to a guy like you."

"A guy like…" He squeezed his eyes shut. "I'm just me. And you're beautiful. You know you're beautiful."

"You're the only person who's ever told me that."

"Maybe to your face." He handed his credit card over, and Cyan studied the graceful way his hand moved, the way he balanced on his barstool.

"I always knew you were handsome," she said. "But it was different when I saw you for the first time in person—not just a face in a painting. You're so much more handsome in color."

"Okay, you're not making any sense. Let me sign our bill. We'll get you home and into… we'll…"

"You don't want to say 'get me into bed.'" She snorted.

Cyan heard him say "thank you," probably to the bartender. Then, she felt his arm around her ribs, lifting her to her feet. "Come on, back to the homestead."

"No, no." She leaned against him. "Let's go to Sea Books. You can see the paintings. You won't believe how many there are."

"Maybe tomorrow, okay? Come on." He led her outside the restaurant and into the bright light of the Charleston Place Hotel. He took a right and pushed through the doors that led to a mostly deserted King Street night.

Strange that, despite her inebriation, she would notice him so quickly: a tall bald man, lingering in the shadows in a long, black coat. He stared at them. Then, she noticed his hands, glowing red.

"Liam." She pointed.

"Max," Liam said.

Max stepped out from the shadows and smiled. "Don't worry, my boy. I'd just like to have a little fun. Sruthán cailleach," he whispered.

"Shit," Cyan said as she tried desperately to regain sobriety despite the way the world had started to spin.

When red light shot from Max's hands, she threw up a shield of gold that ricocheted his spell to a building above. She heard a window shatter.

"Nicely done, little witch," Max said, but his eyes were on Liam. When he threw more red light, Cyan lifted her arm in an aikido block. The red light bounced against the gold that vibrated across her forearm where it was consumed in her shimmering light. She wasn't prepared for his follow up, which hit her right in the stomach and bowed her to her knees.

"Liam," she panted as Max took steps closer. "Run."

Instead of running, he spoke: "You killed Zoe."

Max laughed. "Oh, son, please."

"You were trying to kill me."

Max shook his head. "You've got it all wrong."

In horror, Cyan watched Max throw a whip of red at Liam's chest. She expected to hear him shout in pain, but instead, the street around her was painted in a flash of blue that apparently overpowered Max's magic. More blue resulted in Max taking rushed steps backward, clutching to his face.

When he pulled his hand away, Cyan saw Max was bleeding—and smiling. "Impressive. What else you got?"

Cyan finally found the strength to stand, and she used her self defense training to throw punches of gold light and kicks of glitter, until she felt invigorated by her magic and Max went down to one knee in the center of King Street. She was vaguely aware that somewhere, someone screamed, but she couldn't see any other people on the road. She couldn't imagine their firefight would go unnoticed, however, which was why they needed to get the hell out of there—and apparently Max agreed, because after looking up at a wide-eyed Liam, she looked back to find the dark witch gone.

She took a deep breath and tried not to vomit. “We need to go.” She moved to take a step and crumbled, dizzy with pain and drink. “But you have to carry me.”

Chapter Seventeen

He took her right to Sea Books, closest location of considerable safety. Sybil opened the door immediately, almost as if she'd expected them, which was when she said, "I was expecting you."

"What?"

"I'm a seer, honey." She pet his shoulder and led him to behind the midnight blue curtain where he laid Cyan on the couch.

Cyan leaned up on her elbows and slurred, "Are you okay, Liam?"

"Yeah, ten fingers and toes. Are *you* all right?"

"I feel great."

"But, you—" Liam started.

Cyan turned to her aunt. "So Max attacked us."

Sybil put her hand on her niece's forehead. "Is she…?" She looked up at Liam through red, frizzy hair.

"Drunk? Yes. But it didn't stop her from saving my ass. I-I thought she got hurt out there."

Sybil shook her head. "Doesn't seem it."

"She took some magic right to the gut."

She still had her hand on Cyan's forehead. "I sense no injury."

"That's… huh. Should I call her parents?"

"No, dear, I just told Rue."

He didn't see a phone anywhere nearby. "But—"

Sybil tapped her forehead. "It's a sister thing." She stood and spun around, her hands first resting on his chest and then running over his abdomen and back up around his shoulders. He felt more than a little uncomfortable, but then, she smiled. "You're very muscly. And uninjured."

"Okay."

Cyan curled into a little ball on the ratty couch and snored.

"Sybil?"

"Mm."

"She said something about paintings. Does that mean anything to you?"

The eccentric witch with huge hair who smelled of sweet flowers smiled up at him and put her hand softly on his arm. "Of course, Liam."

"Paintings of me?"

She nodded just as they heard Rue's angry voice from the front room of Sea Books. "Where are they?" The curtain flew open as she walked through. Her palm smacked Liam right across the face with an audible *crack*. "You shouldn't have been out on the streets tonight!" She put her hands on her hips and shouted, "I shouldn't have just slapped you. My anger is misguided."

Liam moved his jaw to make sure it was still in place.

Rue looked to Sybil. "Are they all right?"

"From the smack or the street fight?" Liam muttered.

"They're fine," Sybil said.

Drake lingered in the doorway as his wife spun and knelt by her daughter. She shook Cyan's shoulder. "Has she been… Oh, she's absolutely drunk!" She pointed at her husband. "You! She gets this from you!"

"Honey," Drake whispered. "Why don't you just breathe now?"

Rue took a deep breath in and out and apparently didn't notice that little white lightning bolts were shooting from the tips of her fingers.

Liam took a step back but found the guts to say, "I saw her take a hit from Max, in the stomach. Why isn't she injured?"

Rue lifted the bottom of her daughter's black t-shirt and looked at what resembled a tiny burn mark. "The amulet is supposed to protect her from other witches."

"Maybe not the Dorcha," Drake said.

Then, they all watched the burn mark disappear.

"Oh," Sybil said. "Well."

Rue clicked her tongue. "It heals her. The amulet. That's how it protects her."

"Momma!" Cyan said adoringly, which made everyone in the room sort of freeze. Liam had never once heard Cyan refer to her mother with such fondness. "You should have seen me on the street. I kicked some serious ass. And Liam! Liam made Max's face bleed. I love Liam."

Rue pointed her finger at him, thankfully no longer shooting white lights. "You weren't supposed to hear that."

"She said it to me earlier in the morgue. She said she's loved me her whole life."

"She told him about the paintings, Rue," Sybil said.

Rue's cold gray eyes appraised him. She almost sneered. "Show him."

He allowed himself to be led away from a giggling Cyan, further back into the seemingly never-ending depths of Sea Books. A small room jutted off to the right, different from where Sybil kept her crystal ball. This room smelled like paint and charcoal. He was about to step inside when Sybil stopped him. "Understand they're not all perfect, of course." She twisted a piece of her hair. "I'm not a great artist, and I didn't know for sure if you'd ever see them."

"It's fine, Sybil."

She nodded and led him into the room where he ran right into himself. Well, a painting of himself, anyway.

"When did you…" He pointed at the picture.

"That one? That's one of my favorites. It's from about five years ago."

"Five… five…" He put his hand on the back of his head and stood there, staring, before noticing another picture in charcoal, another in oils—another and another, all of him, all in black and white, filling the entire room.

"I'm a seer, Liam. Granted, I'm color-challenged. I never saw you in color until the day you walked into my shop. But I've been seeing you in black and white for over twenty years."

"Why me?"

"You and Cyan are destined to love each other." She reached out and touched a drawing of his profile. "We'd hoped you wouldn't show up until after the War so you'd be safe, but I never expected you to be a witch, too, sweetie."

"Cyan knew about this the whole time?"

Sybil nodded. "She about died from shock when she pulled you out of that burning car on Broad Street. She went back to the hospital that night to make sure it was really you." She shrugged. "The circumstances are not ideal, but you're destined to love her and be loved by her."

When he wandered, heavy-footed, back to where Cyan lay, he heard her muttering, "He's so much better looking in color, isn't he, Momma?"

Rue ran her hand over her daughter's hair and looked back at him. "You okay?"

He didn't know how to answer that.

Cyan giggled and spoke as if he wasn't standing right there. "Funny thing: somewhere in my head, I always sort of worried that Sybil's paintings were in black and white so we wouldn't know his eye color. Like, he'd show up and his eyes would be…" She pointed at her eyes and laughed some more. "Like the Dorcha."

"What's up with the eyes?" he asked.

"It's one of the only parts in the *Book of Shadows* prophecy that's crystal clear," Drake said. "The Dorcha will have one blue eye and one green."

Liam tried not to throw up. "Is that right?"

Drake nodded.

"But Max doesn't have that."

"A powerful witch who knew the prophecy could do a glamour spell and fake it." Rue turned back to her daughter who was snoring again.

"Oh." Liam hid his shaking hands behind his back. "I'd really like to sleep. In my own bed preferably."

Rue nodded. "Drake, would you take him?"

Despite the yearning to run, or perhaps drown himself, Liam didn't argue.

He and Drake Burroughs walked through the silent streets of Charleston. There were no police sirens, so he assumed what had happened outside Charleston Place had gone mostly unnoticed—beyond maybe a few drunk kids. But what would the police investigate? It wasn't as if light left any evidence.

Outside Liam's front door, Drake paused. "I hope you don't mind, but we had your house put under protection."

"Huh?"

"Sybil. She did some protection spells, made it impossible for anyone who wants to harm you to come inside. Even someone as powerful as Max won't be able to come in if he comes with ill intent."

"Oh."

"You did good today," Drake said. "I'd be half off my rocker by now if I were you."

"How do you know I'm not?"

Drake smirked. "Naw. Maybe a little spooked is all. Get some rest. Get in touch in the morning?"

Liam nodded but couldn't look Drake in the eye.

Once inside, he locked the door behind him and sprinted to the bathroom. The bright overhead lights were practically blinding after his nighttime walk. Liam shrunk back at the illumination but reached forward for his contacts case. With shaking hands, he pulled out one contact, then the other—the colored one. From far away, his reflection looked fuzzy, so he moved closer and stared at himself and the eyes he'd been born with.

One blue, one green.

He'd worn the green contact since he'd been old enough to do so, tired of being made fun of for his "freaky eye." Nobody in America knew about his heterochromia, except Zoe. She appeared behind him in the mirror, as though summoned by his thoughts. No matter that he was half-blind without his contacts; he would recognize her silhouette anywhere.

She leaned against the doorframe, crossed her arms, and said, "Good. Now, you know."

Chapter Eighteen

Cyan woke dizzy to a bloody palm above her face. Flashes of bright blues and reds assailed her memory as she impotently waved at her father's hand. "What are you doing to me?" she asked—or more like croaked. Her throat was dry as ancient parchment. She coughed once before Drake handed her a glass of water.

"How much liquor did you drink, girl?" her father asked. "I've been trying to cleanse you for an hour."

She chugged the water and remembered why she'd been drinking: not only was Liam a witch but also his beloved Zoe was either very much alive or a ghost haunting her. Oh, and then, there'd been the battle with Max outside Charleston Grill, in which Liam had possibly saved her life using his newly developed powers.

Cyan sat up and burped the taste of vomit. "Gross," she muttered.

Drake wiped his hand on the side of his dark jeans. It wasn't really sanitary, the way her father did magic, but he believed blood strengthened any spell—part of his sketchy past, spent meddling with dark magic.

She realized they were in the back of Sea Books, and she vaguely remembered Liam carrying her there. Rue and Sybil had been nearby, too, and then... She gasped when she remembered the paintings. She'd told Liam about the paintings: works of art based on Sybil's prophetic visions of Cyan's true love.

"Where is he?" She moved to stand in the dusty, incense-scented back room of her Aunt Sybil's bookshop, but Drake put a hand on her knee and kept her planted.

"He's home. Resting."

"Home? Alone?" she screeched. "Max could come after him! How could you let him go home alone?"

This time, her father put his hands on her shoulders to keep her on the couch. "His home is protected by spells that'll keep out anyone who means him harm. And frankly, little girl, I think the man needed some space. He had a helluva day, or do you disagree?"

In the course of one evening, not only did Liam learn of his own magic heritage, but his girlfriend's corpse had been stolen from the Charleston morgue, Cyan had then run into said corpse, and Liam had battled a dark witch on King Street before finding out that he was her romantic destiny.

"Okay, he had a long day," she said, brushing blonde braids out of her face. "Where are Sybil and Mother?"

"Sleeping. Everyone is but you and me." He sniffed and rubbed his massive palms together. "Tell me about the fight with Max. Sober."

Cyan thought back. Although she'd been damn drunk when the fight had actually commenced, she remembered it all right, possibly due to panic. "He talked to Liam. He seemed to be *targeting* Liam actually."

Drake nodded. "Okay. What else?"

She compared it to her training and realized something. "It felt like he was pulling punches."

"How's that?"

"When you and I were training at my apartment, some of your spells hit really hard. It didn't feel that way. I felt like Max was just teasing us."

Drake's dark eyes crinkled around the edges. "Why in the Sam Hill would he do that?"

"I don't know. It was actually Liam who drew blood."

"You had a nice burn on your stomach."

Cyan reached for the black agate pendant around her neck—the one that'd been passed down from her Grandmother Plainacher.

"That's another thing: how? This is supposed to protect me from spells."

Her father snickered and ran his hand over his chin, desperately in need of a shave. "Well. I think that pendant is full of surprises. We've come to realize it doesn't exactly protect you from spells, but it allows for quick healing, almost immediate."

"Quick healing?" She touched her stomach—the place where Max had hit her with red light earlier. It felt perfectly fine.

Drake nodded. "Saw it with my own eyes. Talk about an unfair advantage." He smiled.

"So this is real, then. War is upon us."

Drake rested his face in his hands and stared at the crooked, wooden floor.

"Earlier tonight, Mother said you were out looking for answers, talking to other magic folk in the city. Come up with anything?"

He lifted one shoulder. "Some of the older kin, they said they've felt something recently, like something *waking up*. You and Max, I assume."

"The older kin won't fight in the War."

He shrugged again. "Most of them might; some of them will. Either way, I've already called in reinforcements."

"Savannah?" she asked.

He nodded. "New Orleans, too."

Cyan took a slow breath in through her nose. "I'm supposed to lead these people? All these witches who've been practicing the Craft since puberty, and here I am, only had a grasp on it for a couple days?"

"You're the Loach foretold, honey. They know that. They know what your grandmother saw in you. They trusted her for decades, so they'll trust you now."

She leaned back into the comfortable confines of the couch. "When can I see Liam?"

Drake grinned. "At a reasonable hour. It's one AM."

"What the hell are you smiling about, Daddy?"

"I like Liam. I really do. And if we all live through this, I want you to know he's more than welcome in our family."

Cyan rolled her eyes. "If we live through this."

Without his contacts, Liam couldn't make out her face, but he knew it was her. Zoe, *his* Zoe, was alive, right here in their bathroom, despite being declared dead days ago due to a trolley overturned by a dark witch.

He walked across the room and reached for her face, fearing it would be cold but wasn't. She felt warm and soft as she looked up at him. Inches away, he could see her clearly. He blinked. "Zoe."

"Liam."

"Zoe." He kissed both her cheeks and then her mouth, but she tasted like nothing. He wrapped his arms around her shoulders and crushed her body to his until realizing… "Oh, my God, are you hurt?" He stepped back but kept his hands on her shoulders.

"No." She shook her head. "Here." She walked past him and started opening bathroom drawers until she pulled out a glasses case. "Put these on. We both know you're blind as a bat."

He never wore his glasses. They reminded him of his days as a lonely orphan, being called "four eyes" by the older kids at boarding school in Ireland. He wore them now, though, and finally saw her clearly. She wore a tight black trench coat and black heels. Her dark brown hair looked professionally styled. When she'd died in the hospital, her face had been yellow and brown with bruises. Now, nothing.

"I don't understand."

"Why don't we sit down and have a drink?" She turned around, and he listened to her heels tap across lacquered wood. Over the sound of glasses clinking in their kitchen, Liam looked at his own reflection in the mirror. Through his wire rims, he stared at the one blue eye, one green—the only sure indicator of the Dorcha's identity.

It was him.

He was the dark witch they'd been waiting for. Maybe if he'd known about the prophecy earlier? Maybe if he went and told them, told Cyan? Maybe—

"You can't think like that," Zoe said from behind him.

He spun to face her.

She held two wine glasses in her hands, filled with red. "Come sit."

He followed her to the couch. Before they sat, she put their glasses down and pulled his black suit coat from his shoulders. She removed her own jacket, revealing a simple, small black dress underneath, and then took a seat, patting the cushion at her side. Moving as if in a dream, Liam joined her and took the wine glass from her extended hand.

He'd been craving wine lately, so he took a hearty sip and almost choked on the horrible taste. He wiped his mouth as he hurriedly set the glass on the coffee table. "Of course. A time like this, and the bottle is corked."

Zoe froze at his side. "You don't like it?"

He shook his head. "You're dead."

"No," she said. "I'm a witch."

"From what I understand, witches still die."

"Yes." She took a long sip of red. "However, I did a spell a long time ago. After death, I rise like a phoenix. All it cost was my soul."

"Your *soul*?"

"Liam. You're not like the witches you've been spending time with in my absence."

"You mean Cyan."

"And her barefoot mother, crazy aunt, brutish father." Zoe shook her head. "You're no light witch, Liam. You know that now."

Despite the living dead witch at his side, despite her pronouncement, Liam felt oddly calm as if maybe, somehow, he'd known all along. "You knew what I was when you met me in California."

She smiled and bit her bottom lip. Then, she leaned forward and whispered, "I knew what you were the moment you were born. I felt you then, and I've been watching over you ever since. Our dark Dorcha, the one we've been waiting for."

"We?"

"Dark witches the world over. Now that your powers have awakened, they'll all start to feel you, as I did years ago. You were prophesized in the womb by your own mother. She knew what you were."

"Like Cyan's grandmother."

Zoe nodded and relinquished her wine glass to a small lamp table. She leaned closer and rested her hands on his chest. "I love you, Liam."

"What if we go to them, to Cyan and the others? Come clean. Maybe they can help me. I don't… I don't feel like a dark witch. Max is the dark witch. I'm just—"

Zoe pulled away. "They'll kill you if you tell them."

"No."

Zoe stood and ran her hands over her slim hips. "That girl has been waiting her entire life to end you."

He shook his head. "She loves me."

"Good. She'll have her defenses down then."

"Zoe—"

"If she finds out what you really are, she won't love you anymore. She will abandon you like everyone has, everyone but me." She hurried back to his side and cradled his face in her hands. "I will never leave you, Liam. I came back from the dead to stand by your side. I will face the War with you and love you no matter the cost. The Loach cannot say the same. She will kill you unless you kill her first."

He closed his eyes. "I can't kill anyone."

"You would have killed Max tonight for what he did to me."

"Who is Max really? Why did he attack us?"

"He's nothing. A nuisance. You'll take care of him, too."

He pushed her hands away and stood, taking steps toward his front door. "I'm a restaurant manager, Zoe. I run marathons and watch the BBC news. I'm not… I can't be…"

Zoe disappeared from the couch and appeared right in front of him, which made him cuss and take a step back. She held onto his wrist and squeezed until a black cloud began pouring from her palm.

"What are you doing?"

"Hurting you," she said.

Liam doubled over in pain, his chest burning. The pain increased as the black cloud grew. He heard his heart, beat and stutter, beat and stutter, in his ears. The pain was too great for screams. Before his knees could buckle, before he crumbled to the ground and possibly to his death, his abdomen burned but not from whatever Zoe was doing. The feeling of his power was familiar now, after the fight with Max, so he did as instincts bid. Blue light shot from the hand not held tightly in Zoe's grasp, and she flew across the room into their bookcase. Liam sucked in a breath of air and rushed to her.

"Zoe!" He knelt at her side.

She sat up, smiling, pushing misplaced books from her lap. "I'm fine. I was just showing you." She stared up at him and held tight to his chin. "Your eyes are both blue right now. Interesting."

He felt the beginnings of a headache in the back of his skull and closed his eyes before the pain could overwhelm. It didn't. When he opened his eyes again, Zoe—his Zoe—stared up at him worshipfully.

"Oh, one green, one blue. Back to normal." She laughed. "I have no idea what that means. I think you're going to be full of surprises, Liam Cody, but for now, tell me you love me."

"I thought I lost you."

"You'll never lose me." She pulled his face down and kissed him. He hoped she didn't sense his fear.

Chapter Nineteen

Cyan almost didn't expect Liam to answer his phone that morning, but he did, although he sounded understandably nervous after the previous night's utter insanity. Of course, Aunt Sybil had just the thing for that: tea. Plus, considering Sea Books was one of the safest places in Charleston—along with the Burroughs homestead and, now, Liam's condo, thanks to Sybil's spells—it seemed like a good place to meet. Liam agreed to come over in an hour.

Instead of going back to her own apartment—who knew what awaited her there?—Cyan showered in Sybil's tiny flat above the bookstore. She had to dig through mounds of colored fabrics before finding a flowing black skirt and a black tank top, which she accessorized with her leather coat and black boots. She used a pencil to twist and balance her braids on her head but stayed away from Sybil's honeysuckle perfume. There was enough of that wending its way through the shop already. She did light some incense in the back room, though, and brewed a cup of Sybil's Síochái blend that promised peace.

Early as it was, the shop wasn't open yet when Liam arrived. In the back room, Cyan skimmed the *Book of Shadows* prophecy—the one that spoke of the Loach and Dorcha—but learned nothing new. She'd spent her life reading that prophecy, and nothing new ever came of it, nothing changed. At the sound of a knock, she slammed the book shut and walked past the blue curtain to see Liam through the locked glass doors of Sea Books. She smiled and waved, and he returned the favor, although his smile was tight.

She took a deep breath before opening the door. "Morning," she said.

His bright green gaze eyed the doorframe before settling on her face. His lips parted, sort of like a fish, before he cleared his throat and stared at her boots. "You look beautiful."

So did he in a blue button-down and dark jeans with brown dress shoes. He was cleanshaven, and his hair, perfectly styled, just begged for her fingers to mess it up. She puffed out an anxious breath of air. "Come in."

He hesitated on the stoop, staring inside, until he finally took a step across the threshold and paused as if waiting for something to happen.

"You okay?"

"Yes. Perfectly fine." He lifted one eyebrow.

Cyan smiled. "I guess that was a stupid question."

"Did you mention tea? I assume it has hallucinogenic properties?"

She smiled, shook her head, and closed the door behind him before leading the way to the back room, where she'd prepared a tea service and moved two old chairs closer together. The smell of Liam's cologne complimented the spicy musk of incense, the smoke from which had filled the room in a sort of blissful, hazy glow.

"Have a seat." She reached for the tea kettle but not before noticing the way he stared at the strange totems that hung from the ceiling of Sea Books.

"So there's a spell on my house then."

She paused in pouring. "Yes. Just to keep you safe from anyone who might hurt you."

He nodded.

"Knowing Sybil and how she feels about you, she probably cast the spell to last the next hundred years. You might never want to move out of that condo."

He sipped his tea as Cyan sat down across from him. She pulled at the long, black skirt fabric and folded her legs beneath her. "I'm sorry I got drunk last night. Probably the worst thing I could have done under the circumstances."

"Kneeing me in the balls would have been worse."

"Was I mean to you last night?"

"It was nothing." He leaned back in his seat, eyes darting around the room, studying book bindings, spilled herbs, and the incense smoke that rose like a serpent.

"I should have told you about the paintings. Earlier."

Liam chuckled and shook his head. "No. I think working up to that was probably a good idea. It's kind of offputting when a girl you don't know has, like, fifty paintings of your face."

"Do you feel like you know me now?"

"Of course I know you. I might need therapy for the rest of my life because of it, but I know you."

Cyan sipped her tea and held tightly to the small cup as if it might protect her. "Do you think you could ever love me, Liam?"

He closed his eyes and pressed his thumb and forefinger against his eye sockets. His forehead wrinkled, and his breath turned shallow as if his own ribs threatened to suffocate.

"Is that a no?" she asked.

He opened his eyes. She couldn't be sure in the dimness, but she thought they looked wet, red around the edges. He leaned forward in his seat and held his right hand up, palm facing her. As if their magic communicated, Cyan understood. She put down her teacup and leaned forward, too, until her palm touched his. Their hands glowed in a rolling mix of blue and gold, tinged green around the edges. From the tips of her toes to the top of her head, Cyan felt Liam.

"I don't deserve your love," he said.

She folded her fingers over, binding their hands together. "You already have it."

Loud clunking in the front of Sea Books made their hands disengage, and a moment later, Sybil wanderd in wearing a huge, puffy, pink bathrobe. "I thought I heard a lovely male voice." She smiled broadly at Liam, her hair a red rat's nest. "Good morning, you two."

Cyan sighed and leaned back in her chair. Leave it to Sybil to ruin a crucial moment. For a seer, it sometimes annoyed Cyan how blind her aunt could be.

Sybil leaned down and kissed her niece on the forehead. She then pet Liam on the head but quickly drew her hand back with a cry.

Liam sprung to his feet. "Are you okay?"

Sybil shook her hand in the air as if she'd been stung. "Yes. Bad night for you, Liam?"

"Which part?" Cyan muttered. "Finding out he's a witch? Someone stealing his girlfriend's corpse? Or, wait, learning that destiny set you up with a woman you met a week ago?"

Sybil pursed her lips. "It was high time he knew about that, sweetheart." She sniffed the air. "Oh, Síocháin tea. Perfect." She elbowed her way between the twosome and made herself a cup before shuffling back through the curtain to the front of the store.

Liam remained standing.

"I'm sorry I didn't ask. Have you heard anything about Zoe?"

His head shot up, eyes wide. "What?"

"Zoe. Have the police…" She crossed her arms. "Not that I realistically expect the police to do anything, but…"

He stared at her.

"Zoe's body, Liam. Did it show up?"

He laughed and then covered his mouth with his hand. "The police haven't called, no." He then surprised her by lunging forward and taking hold of both her hands. "Whatever happens, Cyan, I want you to know you've meant so much to me—you and your family."

"Sure, I… what do you mean, whatever happens? You're not going to do anything stupid, are you?"

"Quantify stupid."

"You're not going to hurt yourself."

He hesitated.

"Liam?"

"No, I…" He held her hands tighter, his thumbs running over the backs of her knuckles. "I better go home. I have some things to think about."

She chuckled. "Yeah, no shit."

She didn't except him to hug her, so when he did, her entire body weight fell against his chest. He seemed unaffected by her tumble, probably because he was so much taller than her. He wrapped his arms around her body and squeezed hard. Cyan circled his waist with her arms and rested her face against his chest.

"Liam. What's the matter?"

"Nothing." He pulled back and kissed her forehead. He stared at her as if memorizing every line, every freckle.

"Maybe you should stay here."

He shook his head and kissed her forehead again. "I could love you," he said.

"Liam?"

He hurried away. The midnight blue curtain flew like a flag in his wake, and Cyan fell back into her chair with the sound of Sea Books' front door closing. A moment later, Sybil came in, steaming tea in-hand. "Did Liam leave so soon?"

Cyan stared at his empty chair, considering. "Something's wrong," she said.

When the front door squeaked open again, she jumped from her seat, Liam's name on her lips. Instead, she found a tall bald man with a slim box in his hands and a gash on his cheek. At the sight of Max, Cyan's stomach burned with power as she lifted her hands and prepared to light him up like a fourth of July sparkler.

"Wait," he said calmly. "I could not have entered this place if I meant you harm. I had to wait for Liam to leave, but I bring an offering."

"Fuck you and your offerings."

"Stop!" Sybil's voice had never held so much force. She shoved her niece out of the way and approached Max.

“Sybil—”

“Hush!” Sybil, with no hesitation, took the box from Max. She opened the lid and glanced inside. “Where on God’s green Earth did you get this?”

Max bowed. “The great Augusta Plainacher.”

No one used Grandmother Plainacher’s first name—mostly because few people knew it. She was just “Grandmother.” The fact that this dark witch would invoke it made Cyan seethe, but before she could bull rush the guy, Sybil said, “It’s the Plainacher crystal ball.”

Cyan’s eyes never once left Max’s face. “That’s been missing since Grandmother passed?”

He bowed his head. “Indeed. It was gifted to me so that I could keep an eye on you, our prophesized one.”

“Sybil. Call my parents. Something tells me they’re gonna want to hear this.”

Chapter Twenty

Liam stumbled down Broad Street, barely aware of his feet. Cyan loved him, but she didn't know, couldn't know. He wanted to scream, tear his hair out, drink until he went blind. He needed to get back to Zoe and beg for more answers—maybe read the actual prophecy himself—yet the thought of going back to his condo, *their* condo, did not bring peace. He had no longing to run into Zoe's arms. In fact, he yearned instead to rush back to Sea Books, kneel at Cyan's feet, and confess his identity as the dreaded Dorcha. But what would happen then? Would Cyan kill him, like Zoe said?

No, there had to be something he could do to stop all this, to halt the approach of War. Hands shaking, he leaned against the corner of a law office, the plaster cold against his palms. Maybe he could just kill himself—end whatever fate had in store and give the proverbial middle finger to destiny. His wet eyes burned at the thought as he tried to take deep breaths.

"Liam?"

He looked up at the sound of a vaguely familiar voice and recognized the beautiful woman before him. "Layla." She was one of the bartenders at the Bistro, one of the ones who went out of her way to flirt with him at work. He recalled she'd sent an ostentatious arrangement of white lilies to the hospital after the trolley accident, perhaps in the hopes of becoming his eventual comforter.

She put her hand to her collarbone, fingernails perfectly manicured in a shade of light pink. "I'm so sorry about Zoe."

"Thank you."

She stood, staring at him. She put one hand on her slim hip and bit on her plush lower lip. It was well known that the female bartenders at the Broad Street Bistro were some of the most lovely in town, and Layla was no exception with her ample breasts, thin waist, and dirty blonde curls.

Liam realized they stood ten feet from the Bistro's front doors. "What are you doing here so early?"

"Inventory," she said. "Did you know Max is missing?"

Liam chuckled, which was probably the wrong response.

"Nobody knows where he is. Tommy said he even went to Max's house. Nothing. We've all been picking up the slack, since we can't ask you to pick up a shift right now."

Liam's fingers tingled. "Do you want help?"

"Hmm?" She pushed out her full, pink lips.

"Doing inventory. I could use a distraction, to be honest."

"Liam, you don't need to—"

"No, really." He pushed off from the wall that had until recently been the only thing keeping him upright. "I want to do something normal."

Layla pulled the front door keys from the back pocket of her skin-tight jeans. "Okay." She flashed a shining, white grin that promised friendly conversation and maybe more.

Liam followed her inside, the strange tingling moving from his fingers into his whole body. The familiarity of the place—the sights, smells—prodded at his insides like reminders of something dead. No matter how much he'd loved his job at the Bistro, he didn't know if he could find peace there again. The three-story restaurant stood for everything he'd once had and lost, namely, a normal life.

Layla put her hand on his arm. "Are you okay?" She immediately sputtered, "That was a stupid question." She walked away, her cowboy boots giving her walk a sexy sway.

"Will you judge me if I ask for a drink right now?"

She laughed, a high-pitched musical sound. "Of course not, Liam. I don't even understand how you're up and walking around, really. What's your pleasure?" She walked around to behind the bar and leaned her elbows on hard wood. Her breasts practically poured over the top of her low-cut white sweater. "Wait. I know. You drink red wine."

He nodded and made his way closer to her—this woman who meant nothing to him. He shook his head a little at the strange buzzing in his ears.

"Maybe I'll have a glass, too." She spun around. "I've got a Cab open. California. How's that?"

"Perfect." He slid onto a barstool and clenched his fists as she poured.

"Here."

"That's a pretty heavy pour."

She turned back around with her own glass. "I thought about giving you the whole bottle, but…" She shrugged. "You look really good, Liam."

"So do you."

"Is there anything else I can…" She sighed. "Get you?"

Under normal circumstances, Liam Cody knew when a woman was throwing herself at him, and he usually laughed it off. He didn't like girls who tossed themselves at his feet like discarded cocktail napkins—though he was used to it. He thought back to the conversation he'd had with Cyan right before Max's attack, when she'd made his good looks into more an accusation than observation. True, he'd used his looks for personal gain before, but he never did so with ill will. *Did he?* Now that he knew that he was deep down a dark witch, he wondered.

"Can I…" Layla sauntered out from behind the bar until she stood at his side. She ran her fingers through his hair. "Would it help if I held you?"

The buzzing in his ears increased as he turned on the barstool and pulled her into his arms. She stood between his legs and pressed her breasts against his chest. Near his throat, her mouth made a light humming sound before she pressed one, simple kiss against his skin.

They held each other for about thirty seconds before Layla pulled back and looked into his eyes.

She tilted her head. "I thought you had green eyes."

"What?"

"I was wrong, though. Your eyes are blue. Almost like they're glowing."

His fingertips burned. "Do you like me, Layla?"

She chuckled. "Everyone likes you, Liam."

He leaned forward and kissed her. Her mouth was hungry and wet, and his stomach practically boiled. As he stood, he took hold of her waist and lifted her straight up and onto the edge of the bar. She made a pleased little squeak as he did so. He was tall enough to lean her body back over the bar and pin her below him. He held her hands above her head and kissed her throat and the top of her breasts. She moaned his name like a prayer.

His brain shut down as the unfamiliar tingling in his body intensified. He was nothing but animal instinct as he unbuttoned her jeans and pushed his hand inside, his other still pinning Layla's wrists above her head. She bucked under his touch and moaned, begging for more.

Then, his vision shifted. The room took on a deep blue, foggy haze, as he seemed to lift above the scene on the bar. From above, he watched himself let go of Layla's wrists. His hand moved to her throat instead and squeezed. He squeezed until she clawed at his hand. She tried to fight back, but he was too big, too strong, especially when blue light pulsed from his palm. Layla kicked and kicked some more until her legs fell limply over the edge of the bar.

Which was when Liam returned to himself, returned to the sound of Layla's pleasured moans beneath him—and the sudden pressure in the back of his brain. He closed his eyes against the pain, willed it to go away, but the pain fought back.

He groaned—not in a good way—as he let go of Layla and slid back down onto the barstool, holding his head. The tingling was gone, as was the buzzing in his ears.

Layla sat up, panting. "Liam, what—"

The sound of shattering glass interrupted her as bottles along the bar exploded. The young bartender took cover as glass flew, but despite the headache and without even looking, Liam whispered words he didn't know he knew. The flying shards of glass fell harmlessly on top of the bar, scattering like fallen snow.

His headache disappeared.

Layla knelt on the floor and reached out for him.

"I'm sorry," he said as he sprinted for the door.

Although Max was right—he wouldn't have been able to enter Sea Books with ill intent—Cyan still forbid Sybil from giving him tea or hospitality. She made him stand near the point of sales counter, and she stared at him until her parents arrived. Meanwhile, Sybil reverently touched the Plainacher family crystal ball and whispered to it. The occasional flashes of bright pink light lit the room from the tips of Sybil's fingers until Cyan finally snapped, her eyes never leaving Max with his dark eyes and bald head.

"Cut it out, would you?" she hissed.

"You fought well last night," Max said.

Cyan pointed a finger in his direction but kept her distance. "Don't fucking talk to me."

"Language," Sybil whispered, cradling the crystal ball like a newborn babe, which was creepy really. The crystal ball itself was creepy. It wasn't pretty inside like the ball Sybil usually used, filled with light purple amethyst. This ball was completely clear, suspended by what appeared to be a human hand made of copper. It reminded her of Thing from *The Addams Family*.

"I don't like that family heirloom. It's freaking me out."

"It likes you," Max said, folding his hands harmlessly in front of him.

She held up the pendant around her neck. "Crystal balls can't see me."

Max nodded toward Sybil. "That one can."

Before she could cuss him out, her parents barreled in the front door. The fact that her mother had put on shoes worried Cyan more than anything. Drake grabbed Max by his collar and pushed him against the counter so hard the cash register almost tumbled.

"He's not the Dorcha," Sybil said calmly.

"What?" Drake stood nose to nose with Max.

"Where the…" Rue hurried to her sister's side and put her hand on top of the Plainacher crystal ball. The see-through orb momentarily emitted a bright, white light before Rue took her hand away. "Grandmother's."

Sybil lowered her chin as if in thought. "Max had it. He claims Grandmother gifted it to him, and I see no other way that he would have it."

Drake let go of Max, who didn't waver. He still stood strong like a soldier. "Explain yourself, you son of a bitch," Cyan's father spat.

"I'm here to help." Max adjusted his dark suit to its proper alignment.

"By attacking my daughter in the streets last night?"

Max's eyes moved to Cyan. "She knows I wasn't really attacking. I was testing."

"Like you *tested* that exploding trolley on Broad Street," she said.

Max bowed his head. "That was also a test. Indeed."

Rue shoved past Cyan. "Tell me why Grandmother gave you our crystal ball."

"Because she trusted me."

Rue snickered. "We don't trust dark witches in this family."

"I am no dark witch, Mrs. Burroughs."

"Bull shit," Cyan said, and Rue didn't even bat an eye over "language."

"I am a light witch." He lifted his hand like a man taking a pledge. "I swear to you. Augusta Plainacher found me at a very difficult time in my life, following the death of my wife and child, murdered by dark witches to get at me. That was during my life in New Orleans when my name was Maximilian Laveau."

Sybil gasped, but Rue just crossed her arms. "You don't look 'Laveau' to me, if you get my meaning."

Cyan did. Marie Laveau was one of the most famous voodoo priestesses—ever. She was also African American.

Max nodded. "We changed our family name after Marie taught us all she knew as an homage to her amazing art."

"Voodoo ain't exactly light magic," Drake snarled.

"True, but I only dabbled. I stuck to my light magic—which was why those dark witches knew to come for me. They knew I was not properly prepared. I heard about your great-grandmother," he said to Cyan, "and mourning the loss of my family, I came here. She honed powers I didn't know I possessed, which was why she entrusted the crystal ball to me—to keep watch over you."

Rue sighed. "Of course the family crystal ball would be able to see Cyan. Grandmother would have made it so."

Cyan's fingers glowed gold in frustration, so she crossed her arms. "Can we back up a second? We just skimmed over the fact that this asshole killed a bunch of innocent people using a flying trolley as a weapon. Then, he basically shot fire at Liam and me last night. Care to explain all that, voodoo light witch man? Speaking of voodoo, you steal a corpse recently? I know your people are all into zombies."

No one moved to defend Max, so he took a long, slow breath. "People die in War."

"We're not in War," she said. "For the big War, you need a Loach and a Dorcha. I'm here, but if you're not the Dorcha, who the hell is?"

Max glared at her. "Liam Cody."

Cyan was finished with this man. She lifted her hand, palm filled with scalding gold, and was about to just lob his head right off, but Drake's strong hand stopped her.

"Explain," her father said.

"I not only kept an eye on you, Cyan. Your grandmother put a spell on that crystal ball. It would also come to life, no Craft required, when the Dorcha arrived in Charleston. When do you suppose that happened?"

"A month ago," Rue said.

Max nodded. "I saw that boy as soon as he set foot on the peninsula."

"Which is why you hired him at the Bistro," Rue continued.

"Took some finagling on my part to make the timing right. Had to make a man sick, but like I said, War has extreme costs that I am willing to pay. However, as soon as I met Liam, I realized he had no idea what he was. But it would only be a matter of time, with you so close," he nodded at Cyan, "before he started manifesting."

"His eyes are the same color," Cyan said.

"He wears contacts," Max replied.

"No, he…" She remembered, when he was sick, asking for help to the bathroom so he could wash up and *change his contacts*. Her chest tightened. "He does wear contacts."

"I tested him at the Bistro. Small things: knocking glasses over, pushing people down steps. Just my luck that he had excellent reflexes, but no sign of magic. When I met Zoe, I knew she was his pressure point."

"You killed her." Sybil still cradled the crystal ball in her arms.

"Only because *Liam* didn't save her."

"Tell me you didn't steal her corpse," Drake said.

"No, Mr. Burroughs, I had nothing to do with that."

"You killed a woman to test…" Cyan shook her head. She felt sick.

"What I didn't realize is that he needed you, Cyan, to increase his power—your proximity, as evidenced by last night." He gestured to the cut on his face.

"And Cyan needed Liam," Rue said.

Cyan looked back at her mother, whose face was tilted toward the floor as if her whole head weighed a hundred pounds. "He's not the Dorcha," Cyan said. "This is insane. No." She pointed at her father. "You told me if Liam was the Dorcha, he'd have had a dark witch watching over him his whole life. He doesn't have that. He doesn't have anybody."

"She's right," Max said. "I haven't solved that puzzle yet, but I know the young man has a darkness growing inside him—and I believe he is now aware of it."

"What makes you say that?" Rue asked.

Max nodded at Sybil. "He's disappeared from the crystal ball. He's shielding himself, consciously or not. He knows he needs to hide."

"He can't hide when I know where he lives," Cyan said. She walked toward the door and didn't have to look back to know her whole family followed. Before they could even step out onto Broad Street, though, she commanded Max to stay put.

He bowed his head. "I'll follow your orders to the end, Loach."

Chapter Twenty-One

Liam closed the door behind him and leaned his back against it. His hands, although not glowing blue, tingled. He ran them down the sides of his jeans and walked shakily into the kitchen where he found Zoe calmly making sandwiches. She'd changed out of her black dress from the night before and now wore her usual attire: skinny jeans and a puffy, gray sweater that fell halfway off one shoulder. She smiled and extended a plate to him. "Did you say your goodbyes?"

"I'm not hungry."

"You need to keep your strength up."

He leaned over the sink and used his hand to scoop water into his mouth, washing the taste of Layla down the drain. He turned and looked at Zoe—beautiful Zoe—and said, "Why did we fall in love? I don't remember."

She frowned. "Well. That's not a very nice thing to say." She tossed the sandwich and plate into the sink and walked quietly in stocking feet across the living room. "They're coming for you now, by the way, and they know." She lobbed him a sad little smile and disappeared into their bedroom, door closed securely behind her.

"What?"

The sound of a massive fist hitting thick wood echoed in the foyer. Without having to check, Liam knew that fist belonged to Drake Burroughs. He hurried to answer, because the Burroughs family cared about him. They would help him, comfort him, unlike the strange, unfamiliar Zoe who now walked around the shadowed edges of his life.

Liam opened the door and found the hallway outside crowded with not only Drake but also Rue, Sybil, and Cyan, way in the back.

"Hey," Liam said.

Drake moved to charge into his condo, but as soon as his foot lifted to cross the threshold, a floor-to-ceiling barrier of liquid pink appeared and threw him backwards into a wall. Liam stepped away, shocked, and then remembered what Drake said the night before…

"Sybil. She did some protection spells, made it impossible for anyone who wants to harm you to come inside."

Liam stared at Drake, who'd recovered enough to stand straight. "What were you going to do to me, Drake?"

No one spoke, but Rue studied the doorway for a moment before stepping forward with confidence. She had no trouble entering his condo, which surprised Liam: he always thought she'd be the one to curse and ask questions later.

Instead, in her soft moccasins, she stood right in front of Liam and stared up into his face. "Show me."

"I didn't know."

"Let me see, boy."

He used his forefinger to pluck the colored contact from his eye. He blinked and allowed her to see. "Please believe me: I didn't know, Rue."

She nodded. Even though he knew she was gifted at keeping a stiff upper lip, her lip—this time—trembled.

"What happens now?" he asked, hiding his blue eye again behind his green contact lens.

Rue put one hand on his face, leaned in close, and said, "Hopefully. You die."

"But I…" His voice trembled.

She shook her head. "You won't be you much longer. The darkness will take over, and the Loach will take you down." Her hand slid away from his face as she turned and walked for the door. "It was nice knowing you, Liam Cody." She stepped beyond the threshold.

Tears now running down his face, he looked to Cyan and said her name. She rushed around the corner of his building. He heard her boots running on the pavement as she left him.

He didn't wait for the rest of her family to leave. He closed the front door and leaned his back against it before sliding down and sitting on the floor, his head in his hands. He didn't hear Zoe come near, but he felt her hands on his shoulders.

"I told you she would turn her back on you."

He wanted Cyan to hold him—to have *her* hands on his shoulders.

Zoe scoffed. "She'll never touch you again."

"Get out of my head," he whimpered.

"You're the thing she hunts."

"Can I… can I leave the house? Or will they be waiting for me out there?"

Zoe's hands massaged the back of his neck. "You underestimate me. The dark witches of Charleston have been watching you since we arrived, biding their time under my command. Now that War is imminent, they will not let anything happen to you. And let's not forget: I'm much more powerful than I look."

"Will you teach me?"

He looked up to find her smiling. "Most of it will come naturally, like your brawl with poor, sad Max. He's a light witch, you know, hell bent on revenge. He looks forward to the War almost as much as I do."

Liam wiped tears from his cheeks. "Why would you look forward to War?"

"I've had enough of the light witches. I've dealt with them for centuries." She leaned her nose against his and breathed her words into his mouth. "I'm ready for dark witches to rule, my Dorcha, and we'll rule together." She kissed him. She tasted of wet soil and death, and he tried to pull away but she held tight to the back of his skull. "Don't resist me, Liam. I'm all you have to guide you through this. You'll fall apart without me. You love me."

"I don't know who you are."

"I'm your queen. Forever."

As soon as she walked into Sea Books, gold, glittering light shot from Cyan's palm and knocked over a bookshelf. Her father said her name, her mother shouted "Hypatia," and Sybil said nothing. Max stood there, center of the room, holding a cup of tea. She punched him in the stomach.

He grunted but didn't go down to the ground—although the cup of tea was ruined, broken into pieces on the floor. She felt her father's strong grip on her shoulder and shoved him. She faced him chest-to-chest but had to lift her chin straight up to glare into his dark eyes. "What were you going to do back there, Daddy? Kill him? Stab him with your pocketknife?"

"Cyan—"

"You meant to hurt him!"

"Only to protect you," Drake said.

"He's not the man we thought he was," Rue said, stepping up beside her husband. "He's your enemy, Hypatia, who you're destined to fight to the death."

"Don't call me that name, Mother! Now is not the time to piss me off." Cyan's fingertips glowed bright enough to fill the room with what resembled sunrise over the harbor. "And you." She spun on her Aunt Sybil, who picked up a book from the busted shelf and held it in front of her face. "My true love. You've been painting *my true love* all these years, and he turns out to be the man I have to kill?"

"I didn't say it would end happily ever after," Sybil said. "But you do love him."

Cyan threw her hands in the air, which inadvertently brought down little bits of ceiling. "Of course I love him. What's not to love? He's handsome and funny and kind and… *perfect*… except for the fact that he's the dark witch destined to destroy the world!"

Max's voice was not welcome. "Battle arrives swiftly. Light witches already amass in the streets of Charleston. You will kill him, Loach. It's your destiny."

"Fuck my destiny!" The only thing that kept her from breaking his skull was Drake's hand on her wrist.

"Little girl," her father whispered. He didn't let go.

"I hope I die in the War," she said.

Drake looked stricken. "Don't you dare say that."

"I've been closed off since birth, preparing to kill the Dorcha, and then planning to spend the rest of my life with my true love, and now, to win the War, I have to kill the man I've planned for, waited for." She wrenched her hand away. "If my true love, my destiny, is dead, what's the point? Would you wanna go on living without Mother?"

Drake closed his eyes. His chin fell forward against his chest. "My little girl is not going to die."

"If I kill Liam, I won't be your little girl anymore. I'll be an empty shell."

"You are fulfilling your duty," Max said.

"Shut up," Drake and Cyan said in concert.

"Burn the paintings, Sybil," Cyan snapped.

"What?"

"You're not deaf! Burn the paintings of Liam. Destroy them." Cyan started walking.

"Where are you going?" Rue asked.

"Who cares?" she whispered as she stepped into the Charleston morning: cool, crisp, and annoyingly cheerful. She wanted to curse the bright blue sky and tear the swaying palm trees from pavement. Instead, she made her way up Meeting Street. She gave little thought to the people she passed, some of whom looked at her—stared at her. From the way they nodded, she knew they were light witches, possibly new arrivals from Savannah or New Orleans, possibly witches who'd been in her city all along, waiting.

Careless of their support, Cyan arrived at St. Agnes Cemetery and moved down the familiar path that led to Grandmother Plainacher's grave. She stopped in front of the tombstone and howled. "I hate you!" She kicked at the carefully trimmed grass. "You did this! You!" She slammed her palm against the cold stone, which achieved nothing but pain. However, she found she liked the pain. She slammed her fist into the cold marble. She bled, but thanks to the black agate amulet, healed immediately—which only annoyed her more. "Why couldn't I just have a normal life, huh? Tell me!"

The tombstone did not speak.

Cyan gasped for air. "Fine. Have it your way." She tugged at the warm ache in her stomach, pictured Liam's face, and shot gold light right at the stone with her grandmother's name. It broke in three pieces with an enormous crash and tumbled to the ground with the weight of Stonehenge. "How'd that feel, you old crone?" Cyan screamed.

Luckily, there was no one around for her display.

As she was becoming accustomed, Cyan didn't feel exhausted by this show of power. She felt invigorated like she wanted to do more magic, followed by a lengthy make out session with Liam—Liam, who she loved and would never have.

Who she'd probably end up killing.

If he didn't kill her first.

She still remembered the way he'd looked in the foyer of his condo after he'd revealed himself as the Dorcha. She remembered the way his expression had crumbled, his cheeks streaked with tears. She sat down heavily in the dirt and covered her face. He was so alone—or maybe not. Maybe dark witches surrounded him now, taught him how to be bad. Cyan could have brushed off his show of emotion, the horrible dread on his face when he'd looked at her and realized she was not coming to his aid, if she hadn't seen those same emotions when Zoe had died. Liam didn't fake his heartbreak. It would seem his heart had now broken twice. If only she could heal it… but it was too late to go back. They were enemies, to the death. There was no fixing fate.

She looked at the crumbling pieces of her grandmother's grave and, after making sure she was indeed still alone in the cemetery, invoked a pool of gold in her palm. She whispered quiet incantations and slowly, carefully, put the massive tombstone back together until the letters and dates matched. By the time she finished, she couldn't even see where the stone had broken—which gave Cyan an idea, so she started searching the city for her mother. Strange that she knew how to do that now. She knew Sybil and Rue had a psychic connection—"sisters," Sybil always said—but Cyan supposed "Loach" trumped that. She felt her mother's energy at the homestead and took off running.

When she found her, Rue was sitting on the back porch steps. Set up halfway across the yard were a line of teacups, teakettles, and a range of other breakable items. Cyan's mother waved her hand, and a teacup exploded high into the air in many, many pieces.

"What are you doing here?" she asked without looking at her daughter. A teakettle detonated like a landmine.

"Was Daddy really a dark witch when you met?"

Rue pointed her finger, and a ceramic statue of a cat died in a white blast. "Yes."

Cyan shielded her eyes from the sun with a hand over her forehead so she could see her mother better. Rue had never looked so gaunt, her face drawn and eyes tired. "But you saved him, didn't you?"

"Drake made a choice."

"So Liam—"

"Something always bugged me about the *Book of Shadows* prophecy." She mangled another teacup. "Wanna know what it is?"

Cyan waited.

"The two-colored eyes. That always indicated duality to me, like two sides of a coin. Heads or tails."

"Good or evil."

Rue propelled a crystal vase ten feet into the air and shook her head. “Liam. He’s funny. Makes a damn good eggplant Parm. But he’s not like your father, Cyan. The boy is destined to be bad.”

“What if there’s a loophole?”

“You know every syllable of that prophecy. Ever found a loophole?”

“You’re saying I can’t save him.”

“Maybe killing him is saving him.” She reduced a teakettle to dust. “The man you know—the man you know, as he is now—do you suppose he’d enjoy killing someone?”

“No.”

“And yet, he will kill people. It’s only a matter of time before the darkness overwhelms him, creeps up his spine and into his soul. Your Daddy says it feels like a cold blanket has been pulled over you, and the only way to get warm again is to do bad things. By killing Liam, maybe you can send him to his grave a good man.”

“And if I fail?”

Rue opened her palms and let loose a barrage of white light, burning up half the greenery in the backyard. “I imagine I’ll be dead already and won’t care much.”

“You’re not gonna die, Momma.”

“That’s what happens in War, girl. You better start believing it.”

Chapter Twenty-Two

They sat across from each other on the floor of the condo Liam once called theirs but now, he wasn't sure who the woman with him was—this Zoe person. She looked the same as she had before the trolley accident. She dressed the same in pastel business casual, her silky brown hair in a high ponytail. Sitting Indian-style, she rested her hands on her knees and told him to hurt her.

"Hurt you?"

"Well. Try." She smiled.

"I don't..." Liam shook his head. He could see her clearly thanks to a spell that took five seconds. Zoe had healed his eyesight with the power of magic that flowed like a raging black cloud from her palm and over his face. He no longer needed contacts or glasses. When he looked in the mirror, he saw himself, clearly, with one blue eye and one green. When he asked Zoe why she'd healed him, she said it was time for him to appear as his true self to the world. He'd laughed at that. *Who is my true self? Who am I?* Now, he saw Zoe, sitting a few feet away, but didn't understand her.

"Sruthán craiceann," she whispered sweetly.

Liam's forearms burned until his skin actually blistered. He shouted in pain, but instinct made his hands glow blue. In a voice he hardly recognized, he hissed, "Tachtadh."

Zoe started choking.

Liam's arms stopped burning, and the blistered skin disappeared like dirt washed from his hands. However, a moment later, Zoe, searching for air, waved her hand at Liam and shot a cloud of black into his chest. He fell onto his back, clutching his stomach. He felt like he'd been run over by a train—or maybe a trolley.

"Shit," he groaned.

A smiling Zoe soon appeared above him as she crawled up the length of his body and straddled his waist. She rested her hands on his chest and licked her bottom lip. "Do you have any idea how gifted you are?" She leaned down and kissed him. He apparently didn't respond with much fervor, because she soon bit his bottom lip until he tasted blood.

Liam shoved her back with one hand on her shoulder. "Zoe."

She took hold of his wrists and, with strength akin to Cyan's, shoved his arms back against the wood floor. She slid further down his waist and pressed her lower body against his. "I want you right now." She licked a line up the side of his throat.

The way they were pressed together at the hips, she had to notice he was not in the mood. In fact, the feel of her on top of him, her tongue against his ear, made him sick. She wasn't like this—the Zoe he'd loved. She wasn't aggressive. She also wasn't a dark witch. "No," he said.

"No?" She stared down at him. "You've never told me no before."

"This isn't… I can't do this right now."

"Is it her?" Zoe didn't let go of his wrists. If anything, her grip tightened.

"Her?"

"That blonde Loach bitch. She despises you."

"It's not her, Zoe," he said, which might have been half true.

Zoe lowered her chin and rolled off his body. "I'm yours if you want me. Always."

Liam sighed and sat up. He leaned forward and put his hands on Zoe's cheeks. He wanted to kiss her, to feel the way she used to make him feel, but when she looked up at him with dark eyes, he noticed how old she looked. Since when did his Zoe have wrinkles? Since when did her eyes look so cruel? Disturbed, he quickly retreated to the privacy of the bathroom.

Once there, he splashed water on his face and looked at his mismatched eyes in the mirror. He checked his own profile, studied his own face. Did he look different, too, like Zoe? Would he soon begin to warp and whither, become something *other*? Rue told him he wouldn't be himself for very much longer.

"What the hell does that mean?" he asked his reflection, which was when he noticed the priceless glass of wine he'd saved—the last glass of wine he thought Zoe would ever bring him from the night of the accident. It sat on a shelf behind him, but even from where he stood, staring at the reflection, he could see something wasn't right.

He faced the orphaned wine glass. The wine had to taste of vinegar by then, but a smell wasn't what caught his attention. Above the half-consumed glass of red wine, a black cloud hung. Now unafraid of magic, Liam pulled the glass from the shelf and set it on the sink, where he could study it under the bright bathroom lights. The wine sloshed as he set it down, and the cloud shifted slightly, danced.

"What the…"

He stared at the cloud and recognized it. The darkness matched Zoe's magic—the way it poured from her like putrid steam. He thought back to their years together, all the wine. He thought of the night before when she'd poured him a glass, and it had tasted vile.

He backed away. "Oh, God."

When he'd fallen ill after Zoe's death, Rue said he'd been slipped a spell. Even though he'd been half-dead, he remembered they'd talked about him being in state of withdrawal. They'd blamed Max, the easy target, but what if they'd been wrong?

He pulled the bathroom door open with enough force to make Zoe jump, still seated on the living room floor. He towered above her. "How long have you been casting a spell on me?"

She remained on the floor, a look of pure innocence on her face. "What are you talking about, Liam?"

Then, he felt it: a slight tickle in his brain. He slammed the door to his mind as his fingers glowed blue. "You will not invade my thoughts today."

She grinned. *He's so brilliant and beautiful.*

He heard Zoe's thoughts as though she'd spoken aloud.

"You're learning so fast." She used the coffee table to push to standing.

"Answer me," he growled. "Tell me you haven't been… What did you do to me, Zoe?"

"Nothing."

"Tell me the truth!" he screamed, and although she took a step back, the adoring devotion on her face never waned.

Zoe didn't speak.

"You've been putting a potion in my wine."

"I would never—"

He took a huge step forward and held her chin in his hand until she whimpered. "Was it a love potion, Zoe? Is that why I feel nothing for you anymore, because I haven't been given my proper dosage?" He thought about Rue with her herbs and laughed. "Ironic that you can't cook a damn thing, but you can mix up a potion in a jiff."

"No. You really love me."

"I don't." He laughed in her face. "I *really* don't." He let go and pushed her backwards until she almost fell over the table.

"Liam." She shook her head. "I'm yours. I've waited centuries for you, my Dorcha. I've watched over you. I have kept you safe from people who would do you harm. You will not turn your back on me now."

He put one hand on his hip and chewed his fingernail, considering.

"You need my help to win the War," she said.

"Maybe I won't fight. Maybe I'll just kill myself right now."

She laughed. "You think that blue eye will let you do something like that? The dark side of you would never let you die that way."

"I'm not Dr. Jekyll and Mr. Hyde."

"That's exactly what you are, and your whole life, that green eye has been running things. Sweet Liam, desperate for love. A people pleaser." She shook her head. "The first time that blue light came flying from your fingertips, you began to embrace the dark side of you. I've seen it. I've seen your eyes burn blue with dark magic."

He thought back to Layla: *"I thought you had green eyes. I was wrong, though. They're blue. Almost like they're glowing."* That was right before he'd pictured her dead, until the headache and exploding bottles.

"The darkness will prevail," Zoe said, "and you'll need me."

He latched onto her upper arms and squeezed. "You've been working magic on me from the start. What else are you hiding?"

She visibly had trouble swallowing, her nose almost pressed against his. She shook her head and looked away, anywhere but into his eyes.

"Let's see what's in that head of yours."

"Liam," she whispered. "This isn't about just you and me. This is about our people, our dark brothers and sisters. They need us."

"Us?"

"You. They need *you*, but I will call them to your side. Please let me. I exist to serve you, only you." She tried to push up onto her toes and kiss him, but Liam let go of her and stepped away.

"I'm going for a walk."

"I'm coming with you," she said.

"You are absolutely not."

She reached for the cuff of his sleeve. "You could be attacked. Hurt even."

He felt the strong buzzing of power in the base of his stomach that branched through his chest and down his arms like tingles of electricity. "Not anymore," he said and knew it was true.

Chapter Twenty-Three

Desperately, Cyan dug through Sybil's library. She'd always been good at research. She'd find an answer, somehow. She would find a way to save Liam. If there were a chance at duality, any chance in hell that she could sway him to the side of good—just like Rue had done for Drake—she would figure it out. Of course, she didn't exactly know where to start. There were dusty tomes for miles, it seemed. She was familiar with most of them; she was the only member of the Burroughs-Plainacher clan who still used them. But she knew a potion wouldn't work—too simple. Was this hex or curse territory? Maybe.

She swore as she returned a thick collection of gypsy spells back to the shelf and pulled out one about her people's history. Maybe if she looked to the past she could find a situation in which an evil witch turned good? Maybe some ancient story would explain how she could do the same to the Dorcha? She sat in the creaky desk chair, put her combat boots up, shimmied further into her hand-me-down leather jacket, and flipped pages.

"What are you doing?" Her mother, who watched the front of the shop while Sybil painted in back, appeared behind her daughter.

Cyan cussed. "You're the one who told me not to apparate. How come you're allowed?"

"Brushing up on old talents. Preparing. What are you looking for?"

"A way to save Liam."

"In a history book?"

"Maybe it's happened before."

"There's never been a Dorcha before."

She glared. "Can you just let me do this?"

Rue disappeared again. From the back room, Cyan heard Sybil sneeze. She smelled the scent of oil paints and wondered what the hell her aunt was up to anyway. Cyan had already forbid her from painting Liam again.

She thumbed through the thin pages of the aged history book and stared at pictures of witches who'd gone before. There were tales of Salem and beyond. The deeper she dug, the less photos she found but more paintings, etchings. She even came upon a picture of her own namesake, Hypatia: a woman of brilliance and beauty, murdered for being a witch centuries ago. Cyan ran her hand over the picture of a lovely, pale-skinned woman being dragged to her death down the streets of Alexandria. Her hand gave off a golden sympathy glow… or so she thought.

Her hand suddenly moved without her permission and hovered over the book. Pages turned without being touched as if flipped by a strong ocean breeze. Then, the flipping stopped. The page before her eyes, chosen by her magic hand apparently, depicted a painting lush in color and brutality. Cyan was supposed to see something in this painting. She felt the familiar warmth of the Craft spreading up from her stomach and down her limbs, so her gray eyes scanned quickly over the running peasants, the flames, and the dark green of a nighttime forest with an even darker sea beyond.

She looked down at the caption for some explanation. It read, "Destruction of Aunios by the Witch Zosime." Cyan hadn't even noticed the witch, hovering above the townspeople, but there she was, high in the sky. Black clouds surrounded her face, but despite this, Cyan saw the resemblance immediately and shouted a very unladylike, "I'll be goddamned."

"Language," Rue said from the other room, but she apparated at her daughter's side three seconds later. "What did you find?"

Cyan pointed at the painting.

Rue looked, blinked, and said, "Fucking hell."

Cyan lowered her eyebrows. "Language?"

Rue spun the huge book on the desk and stared. "That's Liam's…"

"It's Zoe."

"This portrays an event that happened…" She paused and skimmed the caption. "In the thirteenth century."

"This whole time we've been saying that if Liam was the Dorcha, he'd have someone watching over him."

"Oh, my goodness." Rue put her hand to her mouth.

"Well, someone has, probably his whole life," Cyan said.

"I bet she knew what he was as soon as he was born, just like Grandmother knew about you."

Cyan put her hands to her forehead, which was now throbbing. "But Liam saw her die in the hospital."

Rue put her palm over the painted depiction of Zoe. "She came back."

"That's not possible. Even dark magic, really dark magic, won't make someone immortal."

"Unless she sold her soul."

Cyan swiped braids out of her face. "When I took Daddy to the hospital to save her, he said Zoe's soul wasn't there."

Rue nodded. "It wasn't. The Devil has it. This woman is alive, and she is bad news."

"Will she hurt Liam?"

"Of course not. He's her god. You saw the way Max was looking at you, like you're some kind of priceless jewel. That's how Zoe sees Liam. She'll do anything to ensure his victory, to protect him."

Cyan laid her hand on the pendant around her neck. "Good thing I have this."

"Don't you ever take that off."

"I wasn't plan—"

She was cut off by the sound of a body hitting the ground. Drake and Max were out talking to other light witches in preparation for War, so the only other person in the shop was Sybil, back in her art room. Mother and daughter ran, shoving the door open only to find

Sybil on the ground, muttering. When Cyan touched her face, she was shocked to find her aunt's usually brown eyes white.

"Momma," Cyan said.

Rue took Sybil's head in her hands. "She's just seen something. It's all right, Cyan."

No. It wasn't. Cyan looked up at the painting her aunt had been working on and gasped. It was Liam, of course, but this was not a Liam she had seen before. First of all, he was in color. More importantly, his handsome face was stretched into a horrible grimace, teeth bared. His eyes glowed blue, and his entire face was covered in blood.

Cyan couldn't even get herself together enough to speak, let alone destroy the painting, when she heard Liam's voice right behind her.

She screamed and shot gold from her palms. Liam blocked her magic easily with his blue and then stuttered, quickly, "Wait, wait. I couldn't come in here if I meant to hurt you. Please."

Cyan put her hands on her knees and tried to catch her breath. "Liam."

"Get him out of this room." Rue held her little sister in her arms.

Before Liam could see the horrific representation of himself, Cyan shoved him out into the hallway and proceeded to move him backwards with flashes of light from her hands. He continued to protect himself from her onslaught, but he also continued to back up.

"Cyan. Please!"

"What the hell do you think you're doing here?"

He blocked a shot of gold with his wrist and winced. "You've been researching." He gestured quickly to the books all over the nearby desk. "You've been trying to figure out if there's a way to fix me."

"Yeah, instead, I find out your missing dead girlfriend is actually a several-thousand-year-old evil witch."

"Several-thousand-year-old?"

She pushed him into the front of Sea Books. "Yeah, because her age is the weird part."

"I know she's a witch, and she's not missing."

Cyan put her hands on her hips and waited, staring into the eyes of the man she loved: one familiar green and the other worrisome blue.

"Zoe's at my house," Liam whispered.

"Great. Good. I'm sure she'll help you kill me."

"What? No. Cyan, I came here for help."

"You ain't gonna find help here, boy," Drake said from the doorway.

Cyan hadn't even noticed her father and Max standing there, returned from their afternoon of recruiting—but her father looked downright murderous.

"Shit," Liam said.

"You're on my turf now." Drake curled his huge hands into boulder-like fists.

"Daddy..."

"Nothing here to protect you," Drake continued.

Liam didn't say a word, but Cyan noticed the tense lift of his shoulders.

"Why don't we take this outside? Wouldn't want to break anything of Sybil's."

Cyan shook her head, trying to warn her father of Liam's newfound strength, but nothing could stop Drake from grabbing Liam by the front of his shirt, shuffling backwards, and tossing him onto the sidewalk out front. Before Liam could get up, Drake kicked him in the ribs. Cyan tried to run outside and get between them, but Max grabbed her by the arm.

"Look." He pointed at Liam, whose palms glowed blue—just like his eyes.

"Oh, my God, Daddy!" She pulled out of Max's grasp just in time to have Rue grab the back of her leather jacket and stand in front of her, cautious of the doorway's protected boundary.

"Drake," she whispered.

Liam seemed unaffected by the kick to the stomach. He stood and brushed off his jeans. “You shouldn’t have taken this fight outside the shop, old man. Nothing out here to protect *you*.” He smiled, but the smile was not Liam; the smile was the evil face in Sybil’s newest painting. “Croí pian,” he said. He didn’t even have to raise his hands to cast the spell.

Drake grunted, and his face turned red. He grabbed for his chest and fell to one knee but still found the strength to cast a spell of bright gray light at Liam—which Liam blocked.

“He’s magnificent,” Max murmured, which made Cyan want to gouge his eyes out.

Liam sauntered up to Drake and knelt before him. “You use your own blood in your spells. Makes them stronger, right? Would you like me to cut you open?”

Rue tumbled shoeless onto the sidewalk, arms raised as she shouted in Gaelic, but before she could cast, Liam waved at her. Rue’s hands grabbed at her throat, and she went silent. Cyan dragged her mother back over the protective threshold of Sea Books before she could be strangled to death, and Rue choked on the air she sucked into her lungs. She fell to her knees and grabbed for Cyan. “He’s going to kill your father.”

Cyan shoved Max back from the doorway—Max, who watched Liam with a sort of awe. “Liam!” she shouted. “Liam, this is not you.”

He looked toward her, but his eyes were pure blue.

“Liam, think about California Cabernet or... Connect Four. Remember when we played Connect Four? You were shit at it. Eggplant... you made eggplant with my mom.”

Liam closed his eyes as Drake actually turned the shade of an eggplant, still clutching his chest.

“I love you, I love you,” she whispered.

Liam rubbed his eyes. He looked to be in pain, and she thought about his headaches. Maybe the headaches were more than just oddities. Maybe the headaches were the good side of him fighting for control.

"Liam," she begged.

He opened his eyes, and where she stood, she could see the vivid blue glow was gone. "Get him inside," he said.

Cyan ran to her father and did her best to lift the huge man from the cement. She pulled him through the doors of Sea Books, and he started breathing again, albeit in a heap on the floor. Rue covered his body with hers and kissed his cheeks.

Cyan hurried back to the door and stared out onto Broad Street. The sun was rapidly setting, casting one side of Liam's face in shadow. "I'm sorry," he said, "but I think we're too late." He left her in the doorway as he walked down Broad, one hand still clutching his head.

Chapter Twenty-Four

Liam tumbled through oncoming night, his head pounding with every step. Halfway home, he had to rest, his hand holding to the corner of a house on Church Street. The pain dwindled from behind his eyes but moved into his chest as regret set in, claws embedded in his heart.

He'd almost killed Drake Burroughs. He would have if not for Cyan and her love. Kneeling on Broad Street, he'd felt her emotions—seen them practically like colors on a palette. He'd caught flashes of her memories, images of when they'd first met, images of when they'd first kissed. But he had also been the recipient of Drake's rage like an arrow to the chest, and Liam supposed that emotion was what had done it, put him into a state of defensiveness. Drake had wanted him dead, and Liam had felt it and reacted. He hadn't wanted to stop, which was why, he concluded, eyes suddenly burning with tears, it was too late for him.

He was a thing to be feared.

Before even opening the front door of his condo, he knew there were people inside. Like he felt Cyan and Drake, he felt them, and the feeling made his stomach turn cold. He opened the door, and Zoe rose from the couch wearing skinny jeans and one of Liam's shirts—and the engagement ring he'd bought for her, stashed he thought forever in his nightstand.

"Take that off." He pointed at the ring and paid no heed to the four dark witches sitting in his living room. He could feel their darkness like a chilly ocean breeze. He imagined their evil even ruffled his hair.

Zoe ignored his comment and rushed up to him, pressing a soft kiss against his cheek. "We have guests. They are your soldiers, my Dorcha."

Liam eyed them each individually. They looked normal enough. They didn't wear all black. They didn't have tattoos of skulls that he could see. They weren't covered in blood... or were they? Just like back at Sea Books, Liam saw things he shouldn't. He pointed at them each in turn. "Murderer. Rapist. You killed your own mother, and you put a spell on your neighbor's dog. Out." He headed straight for the bedroom to change. Behind him, he heard muttered voices and Zoe's soft apology.

By the time Liam stepped out of the shower and into an old pair of jeans and button-down, the house was quiet. He was giving himself a quick shave when Zoe stepped into the doorframe at his back.

"We need to get that pendant away from her."

He paused with the straight razor at his throat. "She never takes it off. With good reason. It heals her. Almost immediately. I've seen it."

"Precisely why *you* need it."

He ran his razor under the tap and continued along his jaw. "I told you to take off that ring."

"You intended to give it to me."

"That was before I knew I was under a love spell."

"It may have started that way, but it's not like that anymore. I want to be with you."

"You want my power." He tapped the razor on the edge of the sink. "Which is growing, by the way. Should be able to level a city block by tomorrow."

She stepped further into the bathroom, fingers toying with the engagement ring on her left hand. "And we are all here to help you."

"You've known me my entire life?"

"Yes."

He toweled off his face and turned to her. "Did you know my parents?"

"No."

"But you killed them."

Zoe didn't even blink. "How—"

"You'd be surpsied what I can see now. You made them sick."

"They didn't know what to do with you. They were white witches, Liam, with a prophecized dark witch son. I'm surprised they let you live as long as they did. I saved you."

He nodded and tapped his fingers on the counter, the tips of which burned bright blue. "There was something else you destroyed. I can't see it, but I can feel it. What was it, Zoe?"

"It doesn't matter." She reached out her hand to touch him, but he reached his fingers out and zapped her. She shrieked and pulled her arm away, cradling her hand.

Liam backed her into a corner. "It matters."

Her eyes darted over his face, and for the first time in their relationship, she actually looked scared. "It was nothing. Just a painting."

He thought of Sybil. "A painting."

"Your mother, she was a seer. When you were born, she painted a..."

"Tell me."

"She painted your one true love."

Liam's jaw clenched. "Cyan."

"I destroyed that painting for us."

"But I remember it now." He did—remembered seeing it on an easel in a sunlit library in a mansion he barely knew, his family's home. The memory had been hidden, buried deep, but now he understood why he felt like he'd known Cyan the moment he saw her. "You destroyed that painting *for you*, because you knew I would meet her eventually. Fate demanded it. But maybe if I had enough of your love potion pumping through my veins..." He shook his head. "Get out, and take that fucking ring with you."

"What?"

"Get out!" he roared.

"Liam, you can't do this without me."

"I almost just killed Drake Burroughs. I can do anything I want. Do I need to *make* you leave?" He could feel it, his eyes gone fully blue, and based on Zoe's expression, she saw it, too, and backed away.

"I will serve you until the end, my Dorcha," she said and closed the front door behind her.

With her gone, Liam poured himself a much deserved glass of wine and sat in the silence of his empty condo. Even the city outside seemed hushed. He laughed a little, thought about the razor in the bathroom, and drank more wine. He didn't hear anyone creeping on his porch, so he jumped when a quiet knock broke his bloody reveries.

He tried to read whoever was out there but couldn't. He approached and asked, "Who is it?"

"It's me."

He leaned his forehead against the closed front door. "You shouldn't be here, Cyan."

"Let me in."

He opened the door, and there she stood, blonde braids piled high on her head. The gaslamp on his porch made her skin glow gold as shadows danced over her full lips.

"Are you even able to come in?" he asked, remembering Sybil's powerful spell.

Cyan stepped forward, and he stepped back as she crossed the threshold into his home. The yearning to touch her almost overwhelmed him, so he put his hands in his pockets.

"I can't tell you how sorry I am about today," he said.

She moved close enough for him to smell the scent of her leather jacket and tilted his chin down with the tip of her finger. "She healed your vision?"

He nodded. "She said I didn't need to hide anymore."

"Is she here?"

He shook his head. "And she's not coming back."

"But you love her."

"I love you."

Cyan's gaze moved away from him, toward the floor, and she took off her coat, stepping away to lay it over the back of a chair. "White witches are quickly arriving to help me. Daddy says he's spotted some dark witches, too."

Liam thought about the strangers in his condo earlier.

"We don't have much time."

"For what?" he asked.

She stood in front of him again and reached out her hands. She unbuttoned the top button of his shirt, then the second before he stopped her.

"Cyan."

"I want to feel you before..." A distressed wrinkle appeared between her eyes. "Please, Liam."

"This will only make it worse when you have to kill me."

She pulled her hands free from Liam's grip and continued unbuttoning his shirt. He pressed a kiss to her forehead when her fingers pushed the material apart.

She leaned her nose against the center of his chest. "I'll miss the way you smell."

"I'll miss being alive."

She chuckled, and he did, too, surprisingly.

"God, we shouldn't be laughing about that." She smiled up at him, and her hands ran down his stomach. "Take me to bed."

Liam lifted her from the floor. She felt so small in his arms, despite her immense strength. She kissed the side of his neck as he carried her to the bedroom and laid her down gently. He stretched out next to her with his hand on her hip. "Have you ever done this before?"

She shook her head. "I never wanted anyone but you."

He hesitated.

"You won't break me," she said.

"I was actually more worried about myself."

She leaned up on her elbow and ran her hand down the side of his face. "Why?"

"The last time I gave my body to a witch, it, well... she turned out to be an immortal beast that sold her soul to the Devil."

Cyan smiled and shook her head. "You always were funny."

"You're so beautiful."

She stopped smiling and leaned forward. What began as a gentle kiss quickly escalated as Cyan shoved his shirt off his shoulders and ran her hands over his bare skin. She flung a leg over his waist and clung to him, fingers digging into the back of his neck. She was only so happy to remove her necklace and shirt to reveal a simple, black bra that Liam discarded five seconds later. Both topless, they pressed their upper bodies together. Cyan moaned at the sensation, clinging to his shoulders as her back arched and his mouth found her throat.

He ran his hand over her flat, pale stomach, skin like silk, and touched her softly between her legs through her jeans.

"Liam," she panted.

When he looked up at her, she looked back. Her braids now fell free around her slim shoulders. Her mouth was wet, cheeks flushed. She reminded him of a flower after a rainstorm, dried by morning sun. Liam didn't allow himself to see into her mind—he would not violate her that way—yet a silent question did pass between them, an unsaid, "Is this all right?"

Cyan answered by dragging him up to her by his hair, which made him laugh as he tumbled into her embrace, all lips and tongues and the tantalizing huffs of her breath.

When they were about to make love, Liam lingered above her, hands on either side of her head as he knelt between her thighs. "Tell me if anything hurts."

She blinked several times and nodded, her fingertips dancing across his chest. He loved her like this: not the fated Loach, but a nervous young woman who loved him back. She did wince when he first pressed inside, which made him freeze.

"You okay?"

She nodded vehemently. "More."

They stared into each other's eyes through it all. She occasionally reached up to push sweat from his forehead, to play with his hair. She wrapped her legs around his waist and kissed him—his mouth, his throat, his ears—anything she could reach. He wasn't at all prepared for the sudden deep sound that erupted from her throat or the way her body went taut beneath him, her fingers digging into his biceps. He wasn't prepared either when her whole body glowed gold and filled the room with glittering light. He smiled against her throat as he, too, found completion. His body emitted a shade of bright blue until their colors mixed and painted the room green.

Chapter Twenty-Five

Cyan lay with her head on his chest, their naked limbs tangled together beneath the sheets. The drying sweat on her skin made her shiver, which made Liam pull her closer.

He stuck his nose in her hair. "Just so you know, people don't usually glow during sex."

She smiled. "How disappointing for everyone else."

"I just don't want it to be a let down when you—" He stopped suddenly.

"What?" She ran her hand across his chest.

"I was going to say 'when you have a husband someday,' but a big rock got stuck in my throat."

She lifted her head and looked at his handsome face with its strong jaw, high cheekbones, and soft lips, battered from her hungry kisses. "I'll never have a husband."

He leaned up and pressed his nose against hers. "I want you to. I want you to move on after."

Cyan shook her head. "There'll never be anyone but you."

"You are much too young to say that."

"No one else will ever compete."

"Come on, I'm not *that* good in bed."

She laughed, wrapped her arms under his shoulders, and pressed her face against the side of his neck.

"Then again, I was your first, so for all you know… yes, I am that good." He joined in her laughter and kissed her earlobe.

"For so long, I didn't think you were real. I used to call you my Dof. Did I tell you that?"

He shook his head as she leaned up on one elbow to look at him, play with his hair.

"It's short for 'Dofheicthe.'"

"Gaelic for 'invisible.'"

"Since when do you know all this Gaelic?"

"It just kind of comes to me lately." His hand cupping her lower back made her shiver, not from cold.

"I thought maybe you were some hallucination of Sybil's. She'd sing about you. Someday my prince would come…"

"Snow White?"

She wrinkled her nose. "How did you know that?"

"I am full of useless information."

"And useful." She rubbed her inner thigh against his, which made him practically purr. "Then. I saw you in that wreck. You were real but desperately in love with someone else."

He shook his head. "It wasn't true."

"It sure looked like it."

"You know how we thought Max put a spell on me?"

Cyan's eyes went wide. "Zoe."

"A love spell, no less. The whole time I was with her was a lie. She even killed my parents."

"Liam." Out of reflex, she put her hand over his heart.

"She said they would have killed me anyway. My mother knew what I was. And she knew about you."

"Me?"

"She was a seer, like your aunt. She painted you."

"Which is why you felt like you knew me."

He nodded. "Zoe destroyed the painting and kept watch over me. She didn't actually enter my life until she thought I was ready, I guess."

"Or until you got hot." She tickled his collarbone with her fingertips. Cyan, for some reason, felt no need to talk anymore about Zoe or witches or the War. She wanted to hear Liam laugh some more. She wanted to have more sex. For one night, she wanted to just be a woman in love.

Liam must have sensed this because he smiled. "Please. I was born hot."

She went to smack him on the shoulder, but he grabbed her hand and rolled her over until they were both on their sides, legs intertwined, stomachs touching. She smiled into his kiss and was reminded of the way he tasted like red wine.

"You are very handsome," she whispered.

"You're fucking gorgeous."

"Language," she chided.

He ran his thumb over her bottom lip. "You taste like orange blossom honey. Did you know that?"

"That's a very specific observation."

"It's my favorite kind of honey. I first had it in, um…" He closed his eyes, reminiscing. "Carmel. Right on the California coast. I'd only recently arrived from Ireland. I didn't have a job yet, was just exploring."

"With your endless funds."

He rolled his eyes. "Yes, with my endless funds. I was at a café, and it was crooked. Everything in Carmel felt crooked."

"Sure you weren't just drinking a lot of wine?"

"Fair enough, but the café owner, she was a local. Following the prerequisite jokes about my accent—"

"You have an adorable accent."

He kissed her, tongue and all. She knew it was to shut her up, so she considered interrupting him more often. He sucked on her bottom lip as he pulled away. "She gave me this really strong chai tea, and even though I don't usually drink tea, I said 'thank you,' and she put a huge dollop of liquid gold into my mug. It looked like amber, kind of like you." He put his palm against hers, and her skin immediately shimmered. "I've never had a cup of tea that good, before or since. I used to eat that honey by the spoonful. Haven't had it in years, until I tasted you."

"You taste like wine."

"I'm frankly surprised it doesn't come out my pores."

"It's funny." She shifted closer, pressing herself against him. "I don't even drink wine, but I can't get enough of your mouth." She instigated the kiss this time. She took hold of the back of his head, his short hair tickling her fingers. Despite her inexperience, she knew how to kiss Liam. She knew how to use her tongue to get him to make that deep growl in the back of his throat. She knew how to suck on his top lip until his fingertips squeezed into her flesh. And already, she knew how to roll her hips to make him gasp and whisper her name.

She climbed on top to pleasure them both, his hands guiding her with gentle force. Cyan liked the view. He did have that runner's body—all lean muscle, slim hips, and broad chest. She used his chest to balance herself and although she thought she should feel exposed above him like that, she didn't because he was Liam. He was the only man she would ever love, and soon, one of them would be dead.

Afterwards, he curled his body around her, his front to her back. She tangled their fingers together and refused to cry. She felt exhausted in a way she never had before. With his breath tickling her neck, she muttered, "Maybe this is why I've never much enjoyed sleeping. I never got to sleep next to you."

Hours later, she arose with the sunrise and carefully snuck out from beneath his embrace. She glanced back, but Liam slept on, mouth agape in a silent snore, which made her smile—and then ache inside. This was it. This was goodbye, but she wouldn't say it. Instead, she dressed quickly. She didn't put her boots on until she was outside, and she made her way to the Burroughs homestead where she sensed her mother waiting, no matter the early hour.

When she stepped inside, Rue looked up at her from behind her teacup. She didn't speak.

Cyan pushed her long hair behind her ears and lifted her chin. "You're up early."

"Didn't much care for sleeping." She wore a multi-colored robe. Her light hair was wrapped around the back of her head in a messy bun.

"Where's Daddy?"

"Getting some rest. He was up most of the night with Max, preparing. And Sybil's practically ill after that horrid painting of Liam yesterday. She won't leave her bedroom."

Cyan nodded and felt her mother's eyes on her. She looked up to see Rue staring.

"I doubt Drake would want to see you right now," her mother said.

"Because I went to Liam."

Rue sipped her tea.

"Well, aren't you going to yell at me?"

"I would have done the same thing for your father." She looked again at her daughter, and Cyan wondered what she saw. Did Cyan look different now, after? "Where's your grandmother's pendant?"

Cyan's hand flew to her bare throat. She'd left it on Liam's bedside stand.

Chapter Twenty-Six

When Liam woke, Cyan was gone, which sent him into a terrible panic. How could she… no, she couldn't leave like that, without saying goodbye—without allowing him one last kiss? He threw the covers off and walked naked into his living room. She wasn't there. There was no sign she'd ever been there, in fact. The house was empty, the only sound that of a strong breeze slipping through cracks in the old windows.

"No," he whispered and covered his face with his hands. He rushed back to his bedroom and threw on a pair of jeans before seeking his cell phone, but before he could dial her number, he froze. "No," he said again and put the phone down.

It was better she was gone. If she'd been there in the morning, wrapped in his arms, he might have selfishly changed his mind. He'd made his decision in the night, with Cyan snoring against his chest. If she'd looked into his face that morning, she might have seen it: the decision to kill himself before the War, before anyone else got hurt. She might have looked at him and seen blood.

"No time like the present," he whispered.

He needed to do it, end it, before he spent anymore time thinking about it. Liam was no coward, but he was afraid that if he kept mulling over the idea of killing himself, the dark side of him might talk him out of it. The Dorcha would take over.

Yeah, over my dead body.

He looked around at the beautiful condo he'd shared with the woman who'd murdered his parents. He glanced outside at the way the leaves danced in the late autumn breeze. He vaguely wished it were raining, seemed more theatrical.

Then, he marched to the bathroom and pulled his straight razor from its drawer. He'd shaved with it just the night before, so he knew it was sharp enough. He'd been using the damn thing since he was sixteen; they had a familiarity akin to friendship—the lonely orphan and his daily companion. He flipped it open and stared at his multicolored eyes in the cool metal.

He thought about writing Cyan a note, but she would never find it. She'd never set foot in his house again. They'd had last night, and that was all. Now, he planned to save her with two long cuts along the inside of his wrists. He flipped his left arm over and studied the pale skin, razor blade poised in his right hand.

"Just like ripping off a Band-Aid," he muttered.

He laughed a little until he cried a little, too. He pressed the metal to his wrist and started to push but found his right hand was not cooperating. He tried again to no avail.

"Come on."

He gritted his teeth and tried to force his right hand into submission, but he caught a glimpse of his own reflection in the mirror and stopped.

Both his eyes were blue.

"I told you it wouldn't work."

He spun to see Zoe in the living room, holding a necklace.

"You were right," he said, razor still in-hand.

Zoe wore a summery, yellow dress, despite the cold temperatures. Her long hair fell down free across her shoulders. She looked a lot like she had the day they'd met. "You did well, my Dorcha. You made her forget the pendant."

The necklace Zoe held in her hand was Cyan's.

"You can beat her with this." Zoe smiled. "It will heal any wound."

He stepped toward her and returned her smile. "Let's make sure." He whipped his hand through the air and used the razor blade to slit Zoe's throat. She gasped as he felt blood splatter across his bare chest. He watched her fall to her knees, crimson staining the soft pastel of her dress. He knelt and stared at her, watched her choke on blood, choke on death.

"Don't drop the pendant, Zoe," Liam said calmly. "I don't have time for you to die and come back to life a day later."

She didn't drop the pendant, and bit-by-bit, her gasping slowed. Despite the cascade of blood, Liam watched as the deep wound in her throat pressed itself back together and healed in a grotesque line of puckered flesh. Her blood remained. It covered her, the floor, and Liam, but the wound did indeed heal.

He sighed and took the pendant from her hand. "I guess it does work then." He put it around his own neck just as his phone rang. He didn't recognize the number. "Hello."

"Mr. Cody? This is Detective Schmidt. We met the other evening at the morgue."

"Yes."

"I told you I would keep you abreast of our investigation, and I'm sorry to say that so far, we've come up with nothing. It's almost like your girlfriend's body just disappeared."

Liam looked down at Zoe, gasping and covered in blood on the living room floor. "I guess stranger things have happened."

"I want you to understand how sincerely sorry the city of Charleston is for your loss. We will keep looking. Do you plan to have a funeral service?"

"Soon."

"You know, while I've got you on the phone, I'm sure you're aware that your boss, Max Henny, has been reported missing."

"I heard."

"You wouldn't happen to know anything about that?"

"I'm sure Max has his reasons." He wiped the razor on his jeans, folded it, and tossed it on the floor in front of Zoe, who leapt away from it like a frightened cat.

"You don't say? Money trouble?" the detective asked.

"I'm sorry, but I didn't know Max very well. I haven't been here long."

A loud sigh crackled from the other side. "Well. I'm sorry, son, for all you've been through."

"Thank you, Detective. I hope you have a good day." He hung up and returned to the bathroom. In the mirror, he realized he was a bit more covered in Zoe's blood than he'd originally thought. Thick drops covered his face and surrounded his bright blue eyes. "Gonna shower," he said and closed the door behind him.

Standing beneath the scalding spray, washing blood and Cyan from his body, he thought he might get one of his headaches—any second now—and his eyes would go back to green and blue. The headache didn't come. Liam shrugged and washed his hair and decided he'd wear his dark blue suit that day.

She didn't know what she was going to say when she saw him. After all, she'd just escaped the warmth of his arms a half hour earlier. She'd avoided saying goodbye, and now, she stood again on Liam's front porch. If it weren't for her grandmother's necklace, she would never have returned. Cyan took a deep breath and lifted her fist to knock, but the door opened before she touched it. She took a sudden step backwards. Out of habit, her palms lifted and glowed gold, but she didn't attack. How could she rightfully attack someone obscenely covered in blood?

Zoe, alive, stood in the doorway and observed Cyan. She smiled, and Cyan recognized the woman from the fridge photo—the lovely lady in a pastel yellow summer dress when she should have been wearing a sweater and jeans. Well, she should have been clean of blood, but she wasn't. Her dress was covered in dark red, as was her bare throat and the bottom of her face. Swatches of crimson painted her knees and her right hand, which held a sponge as though she'd been cleaning—cleaning what looked to be a large pool of blood on Liam's floor.

Cyan panicked and shoved inside the condo. "What did you do to Liam?"

"Oh, he's just getting dressed."

"What?"

"He's getting dressed." Zoe, as if in a trance, turned back to the pool of blood, a bucket of pink water nearby, and kept sopping up bodily fluids from the wood floor.

"Liam?" Cyan called.

His bedroom door opened, and his head poked out. He was busy adjusting his tie over a light blue shirt. "Cyan. I thought I heard your voice."

She tried not to look at Zoe, scrubbing away. "What's going on?"

"Oh. You left your pendant." He gave her a tight-lipped smile. "I was just testing its healing abilities on Zoe. Isn't that right, babe?"

"Mm-hmm," Zoe hummed.

Liam patted his chest. "I'm going to hang onto it. Hope you don't mind."

Cyan shook her head in confusion. She moved to touch him, reach out and clasp hands, but she pulled back when she looked into his eyes and saw unfamiliar blue—both of them. "Liam?"

"I'm glad you came back, Cyan. I wanted to thank you for last night. It had been so long since I'd fucked a virgin."

Zoe snickered.

"Your inexperience was adorable." He put a strong hand on the back of her head and kissed her forehead. "And you got so wet over that story about the honey." He sighed. "But I will miss the way you throw yourself at me."

She stared up into unfamiliar eyes. "What happened to you?"

"Oh, well, I was going to kill myself after you left this morning, and… you know, I can't remember why." He shrugged. "I feel really good right now, though. Could be the virgin sex."

"Poor little virgin," Zoe sang off-key.

"Liam, this isn't you."

"But it is me. All my life, I've been trying to figure out who I am. I've looked for answers in other people, in places. In love. But I was born with the answers. I just needed to meet you to figure it out—you, the Loach." He licked his upper lip, and Cyan hated that she knew what he tasted like. "You won't be quite as effective without your grandma's jewelry. Let's see you take me down in the War now."

Her hands curled into fists. "You'll die at my hand."

"Maybe." He tilted his head. "But I'll be sure to take you with me."

She watched him walk back to his bedroom, humming. Before she could leave, Zoe appeared in front of her again, dark eyes wide. She slowly, slowly reached out her bloodstained fingers and caressed Cyan's chin. "I can hurt you now, Loach." She laughed.

The entire walk to Sea Books, Cyan felt eyes on her. People watched from the shadows—not people but witches. She was no longer protected by her grandmother's magic, and the realization made her palms tingle with defensive magic. She avoided eye contact and hurried on her way until she pushed into Sea Books and closed and locked the door behind her. Cyan followed the well worn path to her aunt's art studio, and yes, there it was: the last painting Sybil had done of Liam, the man covered in blood with eyes of clear, cruel blue.

Cyan picked up the painting and broke it over her knee. She howled as she tore the canvas to pieces and then crumbled to the floor amidst the remnants. She didn't hear Sybil approach, but she turned at the quiet whisper of her name and the scent of honeysuckle.

Her aunt was wrapped in a wool afghan of many colors. She looked tired and worn but, more than that, sad. "We've lost him," Sybil said. "That beautiful boy."

Cyan felt the tightness of dried blood on her chin, leftover from Zoe's unwelcome touch. She clawed at the residue with her own short nails.

"He was very kind. Funny, too."

"I have to kill him." Cyan stared down at her hands. "B-but he has grandmother's pendant. I don't know if I can."

Sybil carefully sat on the floor beside her niece and brushed blonde braids from Cyan's face. "His child is within you," she said. "I see it already."

Cyan laughed—a cold, awful sound.

"She will have a long life."

Cyan glared. "Don't make shit up, Sybil."

"I'm not making shit up." The foul word sounded foreign from Sybil's mouth. "I *see*."

"I wish you'd never seen Liam."

"It would have happened anyway. You were destined to love him. I only painted so many pictures because he was very nice to look at."

Cyan thought of his freakish bright blue eyes. "Not anymore."

A commotion at the front of the shop brought them both to their feet. Someone banged on the locked door.

"It's your father."

"It's my father."

Cyan left Sybil still planted on the floor in the back room and heeded Drake's call. He stepped past her and into the store, followed by Max and a handful of others—light witches. Drake refused to look at his daughter until she finally said, "Daddy?"

"They've sent out a call," Max said. "Dark witches are pouring into Charleston. The War begins tonight." He practically grinned.

"Where?" Cyan said.

Her father nodded toward the door. "Center of Broad Street."

She grabbed him by the arm and dragged him away from the others. "I will not go into battle with you angry at me."

He dragged her further into the store. "You shouldn't have gone to him."

"Mother would have done the same for you—if only to say goodbye."

His chin shook as he looked away from her.

"Daddy." She took his hand gently. "I had to. And now it's done, and now, he has to die."

"Will you be able to kill the man you love?"

She thought about the blue-eyed monster in the French Quarter. "He's not the man I love anymore. The Liam we knew is gone."

Drake pulled her into a tight embrace. "My little girl."

"He's mine to kill," she said against his thick jacket. "Nobody else."

Her daddy nodded. "Yes. He's yours."

Chapter Twenty-Seven

The Plainacher pendant felt warm beneath his shirt against the bare skin of his chest as he used his blue magic to spin a fork on the coffee table in his living room. The house bustled with dark witches, some having arrived from as far away as California—members of a coven Zoe once knew during their time in San Francisco. There were locals, too, though: the girl from a coffee shop on upper King who knew to leave Liam's coffee black; a bartender from Charleston Grill who knew Liam preferred California Cabernet; and even Tommy, the sous chef from the Bistro.

When he'd walked in, he'd tried bowing to Liam, but Liam had instead given the young dark witch a hug, ruffled his hair, and said, "You're still short."

He did his best to nod to the witches who entered his home—witches who would have been unable to enter if they meant him harm. They did not. He could tell by the way they watched him, they hoped to worship him. He was their leader who would kill the light witches of Charleston and those of the next city, the next, until the world was peopled with only their kind. Maybe he would sell his soul like Zoe and live forever in the Devil's grip. The thought thrilled him.

Zoe flitted about, greeting newcomers, pouring wine. She had on a long, dark green gown Liam had never seen that looked like something out of a Grimm Fairy Tale. Vacant were her pastels and summer dresses. He assumed this was her battle gear. Her brown hair hung long and straight down her back. When she walked, clouds of thick black crept from beneath her gown, enveloping the floor in smoke. Her powers overflowed.

Liam felt a similar fullness. His stomach was warm and fluttering. He could barely keep his fingers from glowing deep blue. Battle beckoned, and his innate abilities, recently awakened, were so strong he heard thoughts like spoken words as dark witches rehearsed their favorite spells—best for decapitation, best for throwing fire… best for horrible, bloody death. He had a list in his own head, as well, and he almost smiled with their familiarity, as if he'd always been this dark thing inside.

"It's almost time," he whispered, and the whole room fell silent. Liam stood and ran his palms down the front of his suit. "I take this opportunity to thank you all for being here."

There were muttered thanks, but most averted their gaze as though scared to look at him—as though he was something royal, something godly.

"We go to battle. The Loach will be destroyed, and with her, her people. I make one demand, and the witch who does not follow my demand will die." He paused. "The Loach is mine to finish."

Zoe bowed in front of him. "We will keep you protected as you tear her apart, my Dorcha."

He ran his finger along the edge of her jaw. "I owe you."

"You owe me nothing. It has been my honor." She bowed lower as she backed away, and Liam looked at the twenty or so dark witches amassed in his living room. They stood at the ready, including young Tommy who grinned as he shot orange light from one of his fingers to the next.

"We're ready," Liam said. "Let's go to War."

Zoe shielded them for the walk to Broad. Although it was almost midnight, there was no need for a curious tourist to see a mismatched band of dark witches walking the streets of Charleston. All of Broad Street was shielded, as well. No one of the non-magical variety would be able to enter the street until the battle was over. No sounds would escape, not even screams. The city would be none the wiser of a centuries-old prophecy coming to its conclusion.

Liam saw them a block down Broad Street as soon as he turned the corner: Drake, Rue, Sybil, Max, and many others he didn't recognize, with Cyan in the center. Her bright blonde hair glowed in the moonlight, and the rest of her—the leather jacket, the jeans, the boots—matched the blackness of night. There were others that Liam knew from local businesses, all light witches who wanted him dead.

Well. That wasn't happening.

"How nice to see all of you." His voice echoed down the thin, palm tree-lined corridor. He gave a single thought to the trolley accident—the start of this.

"You have to die, Liam," Cyan shouted.

"Back at you, honey lips." He smiled when he noticed Drake visibly tense at his daughter's side. "Shall we?"

Knowing her as well as he did, he wasn't surprised when Cyan didn't hesitate. A streak of gold light, accompanied by a Gaelic curse, flew down the center of the street until he blocked it, caught it in the blue light of his hand. By then, though, their gold and blue magic was not alone. Shining lights of pink, silver, red, black… a horrific rainbow cascaded in arches and line drives back and forth. Despite the occasional scream, Liam paid no mind to the others. His blue eyes focused solely on Cyan who ran at him with great speed. Ten feet between them, she stopped and started throwing curse after gold-colored curse. She moved like the martial artist that she was, hurling spells like punches and kicks.

He felt the heat of her magic a couple times but was able to block all of it before she caused any permanent harm. Besides, he had her grandmother's pendant. Even if she landed a good hit, he would heal—unlike Cyan.

"Dealanach bás," Liam snarled, prepared to watch her slim body fall to the ground in an inferno of death.

She groaned as she blocked that one, possibly feeling its weight, and their fight paused long enough for her to gape at him, shocked at what he'd just thrown. It was almost as though she only just realized he truly did mean to kill her.

Cyan howled, and although there was no gold light, he knew he needed to prepare. People moved around him like shadows, some at speeds no human could fathom. He heard Zoe shouting from on high as she floated ten feet above his head, suffocating light witches in her tumultous clouds of black. She was just full of surprises.

In front of him, Cyan pulled in a deep breath of air and then, promptly, vanished.

"Shit," Liam said, but he soon sensed the arrival of magic behind him like the tickle of static electricity. He began to turn but felt her hand digging into his shoulder as she began shouting a spell—and then, she screamed. She choked on air as her hand fell away. He heard her body hit pavement, and he turned. Cyan lay on the ground, hand to her chest, gasping for breath. Her gray eyes opened wide as she stared up at him, and Liam's head began to ache.

"No," he said, just as Zoe cackled from above.

"For you, my Dorcha! For you!"

He didn't think, didn't consider his options, as he stood there watching the famed Loach die. He held his palm toward Zoe and whispered, "Téigh go dtí ifreann." He watched the woman he'd loved, his lifelong protector, as her feet turned to ash, then her legs. Zoe didn't scream when she realized what he'd done. Instead, she stared at him, eyes disbelieving. She shook her head and blew away in the breeze like the final embers of a nighttime house fire.

"Cyan." He knelt beside her and put his hand on her cheek.

Her lips were tinged red with blood as she looked up at him. "Your eyes are blue and green again."

He tore open his shirt, pulled the pendant from around his neck, and pressed it to her chest. She groaned at its arrival as if the healing hurt, but she was healing—he could feel it. Whatever curse Zoe had lobbed was soon sucked into the black agate as Cyan began to breath normally. The blood even disappeared from her lips. Then, she sat up and wrapped her arms around him. He buried his face against her neck, no longer caring about murder and War. If only they could run away. Couldn't they just run away?

He thought about asking her to make them vanish, as she'd done for herself but moments earlier. However, before he could speak, he heard her shout. Then, he felt the pain.

"No," Cyan shrieked.

Max, a few feet away, grinned in victory, the red light of his magic still dancing across his hand. She zapped him, sent him flying onto his back, and waved her arm in the air. A golden dome surrounded she and Liam—Liam, who was paler than a piece of paper, who wheezed and fell out of her arms onto his back, gasping, gasping.

She leaned over him and ran her hands over his face. "Liam. Look at me."

His eyes seemed to search for her, but she wasn't sure what he saw anymore. She was sure, however, that his eyes no longer glowed blue. She was also sure he'd just saved her life. She turned around and searched the pavement until she found the Plainacher pendant. She tried to press it against his skin, but Liam stopped her.

"Let me go."

"No." She shook her head and pushed the amulet closer, but his hand kept her away.

"I just tried to burn you to death."

"That wasn't you."

"It was me. I did it. I remember doing it." He coughed on a breath. His chest shivered as his eyes filled with tears. "That was a hell of a spell. This hurts."

"No, no, you can't go." Her own vision blurred with saltwater as she took his hand and held it to her stomach. "Sybil says there's a baby. She's gonna need her daddy."

He seemed at a loss for words, either from shock or from the fact that he was dying. "Will you kiss me, please?"

Their kiss tasted like salt and the thick iron of blood. She didn't dare try to take his pain away, certain it would kill her and their unborn child. She kissed him as if they were just two young people in love. She tried to tell him how much she loved him in that kiss, and she did feel something—a pull of her magic, a push of his, until the safe interior of their golden orb glowed green. The air glowed and glowed, even when Cyan pulled away and wrapped Liam in her arms.

She kissed the side of his head. "Be my husband. Be a father. Please."

"Did you just propose to me?"

She pulled back and smiled through her tears. "Liam. Your eyes are both green."

He sat up. "I'm not dying anymore either."

She put her hands on his cheeks and stared at him. The color was back in his skin. He didn't look weak. He looked strong as Drake Burroughs, but his eyes were the most amazing things—bright, clear, emerald green. "You healed yourself."

"Apparently I'm doing that now."

"How?" That single word held a dozen questions.

"Well, I always wanted a family." He stood and pulled her with him. They watched the battle still raging around them but then slow as witches saw the two of them, alive, together. He glanced down at her. "I need to kill a bunch of bad people. Is that okay?"

"Um, yeah."

He gave her hand a squeeze. "You're going to have to drop the shield."

"Right. When I do, I'm going to stand right behind you and keep you safe."

"You're going to fight your own family?"

"For you." She nodded.

Liam took a deep breath and exhaled slowly. "Ready?"

"Ready."

"Wait." His eyes searched the ground until he found her grandmother's pendant. "Put this on."

"You might need it more than me."

He put the necklace around her neck and clasped it. "We've got a baby to worry about." He kissed her forehead. "Okay. Let's do this."

Cyan dropped the shield, and she'd been right to stand by Liam. Her father charged until she gave him just a little push that sent him onto his back. Max was next, tossing red flares like a whip. She wanted to get their attention, tell them to stop, but it was Sybil who took care of that. Her aunt had a bit of blood on her face. Her red hair was a tangle, and her long skirts were torn. However, she was a seer, and she saw.

"Stop!" she said, and she threw a pink wall between Cyan and the light witches.

Behind her, an unfamiliar voice: "Dorcha, do we fight?"

"Sorry, Tommy," Liam said, "but you picked the wrong side."

Cyan turned to watch as Liam's hands glowed not his usual blue but a deep green like his eyes. She took a step back and yelped when she felt arms around her. "You fixed him," Rue said.

"We fixed each other."

The green light grew brighter, and some dark witches began to run, but there was no time. The words reverberated down the corridor of Broad Street and up the sides of buildings: "Luaithreach a luaithreach."

Like Zoe, every dark witch began turning to ash. The night filled with screams. Some pointed accusatory fingers, damning the Dorcha—their supposed leader, now murderer. Legs turned gray as though consumed by invisible flame. Torsos tumbled, fingers scraping concrete. Faces twisted into grimaces of hate and horror. Then, the wind blew. The ashes swept across the street like dead leaves and disappeared down sewers and up darkened alleys. Liam's hands stopped glowing.

Slowly, the great Dorcha turned around and said, "I need a drink."

Chapter Twenty-Eight

With Christmas soon to arrive, the entire city of Charleston was covered in big, red bows and white twinkle lights. Apparently, her father felt the Burroughs backyard needed similar treatment as Cyan and Rue sat on the back patio, watching Drake do his best to untangle a string of multi-colored mini-lights. He grumbled until Liam, laid out in the hammock, waved his hand. The string jumped out of Drake's hand—which made him cuss—untangled itself in the air, and came to rest, organized, on the edge of a bed of mulch.

Cyan smiled.

"He's more powerful than any witch I've ever seen," Rue said.

"Because he can untangle Christmas lights?"

"You know what I mean."

"It scares him sometimes," Cyan said.

"It's a good thing he's got you."

"It's a good thing we've got each other."

Rue hummed in agreement as Sybil arrived with a pitcher of sweet tea. "Is the young man tired today?"

"Long night last night at the Bistro. Some fancy fundraiser. He didn't get home until around three. Not that I was sleeping." Cyan still had trouble sleeping unless Liam was with her, and he was quite busy and important now as the new owner of Broad Street Bistro.

After the War, Max left town, although not immediately. First, he tried talking Drake and Liam into a nationwide hunt. The dozen or so dark witches Liam had taken out weren't enough, according to Max. Still hell bent on revenge for his family's murder, he was hungry for more blood. Although Liam had listened silently, Drake had spoken up pretty fast. In fact, Drake suspected Max had a bit more darkness in him than he dared admit, in part due to his voodoo past. Cyan's father had yet to forget the amount of power it would have taken to flip that trolley all those weeks ago. Like Zoe, Max might have sold his soul for power like that, and Drake wanted nothing to do with him, which meant Liam didn't either. Drake had become Liam's advisor in all things magic, really, so he listened when Cyan's daddy said no, so Max left—and Liam bought the Bistro with money from his inheritance.

"You need to be sleeping." Sybil sat down and eyed Cyan's stomach meaningfully.

"I sleep enough." She watched Liam roll onto his side in the hammock. His hair was getting longer, and the dark locks curled around the edges of his forehead. He itched his nose and looked to be sleeping again ten seconds later.

"You're going to be wonderful parents." Sybil grinned.

Cyan rolled her eyes and played with her grandmother's pendant around her neck. "You keep saying that. I've never even changed a diaper."

Rue scoffed. "You're a witch. Figure it out."

An enormous cuss word broke up their conversation, and Drake tossed the Christmas lights into the grass.

"Language," Rue said.

"One of the damn bulbs is out," her father muttered.

"Do I have to do everything?" Smiling, Liam rolled out of the hammock and walked barefoot across the backyard. He put his hand on Drake's thick shoulder and said something that made her daddy laugh. She liked when Drake and Liam got along, because they didn't always. Sometimes, her father didn't want to see him. Sometimes, she caught him watching Liam like he wanted to hurt him—or at least like he didn't trust him. Liam's eyes had been green ever since the War. His magic had glowed green, too, no longer that vibrant blue that bespoke bad tidings. Maybe Drake would move on eventually—forgive Liam—but maybe not.

Liam's immense power didn't help. Once things had settled down, Cyan had worried about Zoe coming back. After all, she'd sold her soul for immortality; it was only a matter of time before she showed up again.

Then, one day, Liam had said, "She's not coming back."

"How do you know?"

"I sent her to Hell."

There'd been a long pause around her family's dinner table until Rue had said, pleasantly, "Oh."

Rue was right: Liam was the most powerful witch any of them had ever heard of, which rightfully caused a bit of tension at times. There was no telling where his capability ended, but despite this, Liam didn't use magic very much. The only times he used his abilities were to be helpful or to make Cyan laugh. He did glow green in the bedroom, but that wasn't on purpose. That just sort of happened. At least the headaches were gone.

The boys finished decorating just in time for sunset. As the sky burned colors of bright pink, orange, and finally purple, the Burroughs homestead glowed gently, tiny twinkle lights curled through bushes and trees. Rue and Sybil oohed and congratulated Drake on a job well done as Liam pulled Cyan to the hammock. They lay together side-by-side with her face on his chest, his fingers in her hair.

"Thanks for helping Daddy."

"Mm."

"You feel okay?"

"I'm in a hammock with my pregnant wife. I feel perfect."

They'd gotten married only the week before in a simple ceremony on the harbor, so it still made her stomach twitch with happy butterflies whenever he called her "wife." For the wedding, she'd worn her leather jacket over a simple, black dress. Liam had worn a light gray suit—handmade and from London, of course. She hadn't realized quite how many suits her husband owned until he'd moved into her tiny apartment on East Bay. It was a temporary arrangement, though.

Liam wanted to buy her a house so they could have a garden and more space for the baby.

"How often do you feel her?"

She lifted her head. "Hmm?"

"You know she's growing." He put his hand on her stomach. "But how often do you notice?"

"Not very often."

"I wonder what she'll be like."

"I've forbid Sybil from doing any readings."

He chuckled against her forehead, his breath, as usual, smelling of vanilla and oak. "And definitely no paintings."

"No. No paintings."

"I hope she looks like you." He held her tighter against him, and she wrapped her arm around his slim waist.

"Is this what happily ever after feels like?"

"I think so," he whispered. He lifted his hand until she pushed her palm against his. They lit up the night with flickers of glittering gold and emerald green until the night turned to day. The darkness turned to light.

ABOUT THE AUTHOR

Sara Dobie Bauer is a bestselling author, model, mental health speaker, and LGBTQ advocate with a creative writing degree from Ohio University. Twice nominated for the Pushcart Prize, she lives with her hottie husband and two precious pups in Northeast Ohio, although she'd really like to live in a Tim Burton film. She is author of the Bite Somebody series and Escape Trilogy, among other ridiculous things.

Learn more at http://SaraDobieBauer.com.

Photo credit: Bill Thornhill

Thank you!

Thank you for reading

DESTINY'S DARK LIGHT

We would appreciate it a great deal if you would leave an honest review on Goodreads and wherever you bought this book!

Made in the
USA
Lexington, KY

54426054R00141